THE JUDEAN

STORIES FROM BETWEEN THE LINES OF SCRIPTURE

CHRONICLES

D1013649

THE JUDEAN

STORIES FROM BETWEEN THE LINES OF SCRIPTURE

CHRONICLES

DON PATE

REVIEW AND HERALD® PUBLISHING ASSOCIATION
HAGERSTOWN, MD 21740

Copyright © 1997 by
Review and Herald® Publishing Association
International copyright secured

The author assumes full responsibility for the accuracy of all
facts and quotations as cited in this book.

This book was
Edited by Gerald Wheeler
Interior designed by Patricia S. Wegh
Cover designed by Matthew Pierce
Photo illustration by Matthew Pierce
Typeset:11/12 Weiss

PRINTED IN U.S.A.

01 00 99 98 97   10 9 8 7 6 5 4 3 2 1

R&H Cataloging Service
Pate, Don, 1951-
      The Judean chronicles: stories from between
the lines of Scripture.

      1. Bible stories.   I. Title.

            220.9

ISBN 0-8280-1253-9

DEDICATION

I will never forget that for more than five years you were a wonderfully supportive "boss" and friend. Then, when the going got really tough (and none of it was your fault at all!), you were an even better friend. In spite of it all, you sought to work for my *true* best interest in every way.

I can't comprehend that there would be many who would choose to believe that someday the smoke could clear and that God was capable of causing "all things to work together for good."

Wayne Longhofer, I owe you, and always will.

CONTENTS

NAHUM, THE POTTER

If you travel the Golan today, you will see remnants of un-counted wars. In the days of Elisha Syrian armies rolled down these heights into the headwaters of the Jordan and on to the region of the Galilee. Invading forces muscled their way into the region throughout the period of the Old Testament monarchies. A thousand years ago the Crusaders and Muslims built forts here to defend the land, and those abandoned citadels still dot the countryside.

A monument alongside Israeli Highway 99 honors a farmer/tank commander who, for hours, singlehandedly held off more than a dozen enemy tanks when Israel repelled attack from all sides on Yom Kippur, 5733/1973. When this farmer heard the heart-stopping sirens he knew (as all men and women of Israel know) where his duty station was to protect the land. Driving his tank to the brow of the hill, he saw the joint Lebanese/Syrian/Jordanian force climbing the ridge in front of him. By an amazing act of stealth and courage, he bluffed the approaching tank force. Hour after hour he maneuvered his tank below the ridge, each time topping the hill from a different position. The invading soldiers believed they were facing a formidable line of Israeli tanks hiding just below eye level. One lone, committed farmer held his ground until reinforcements from the Galilee floor arrived to begin a counterattack. Had that invading force made it to the Jordan River, it would have been but a hop, skip, and jump to Jerusalem. That simple farmer/tank commander is an Israeli hero to this day. The sculpture of a tank canopy welded to a metal tractor tire remembers his bravery and commitment.

The Judean Chronicles

Behind the roadside monument you may wander through bunkers that still contain ammo boxes, shells live and spent . . . all reminders of the strategic importance of the Golan in Israel's history throughout untold generations.

Part I

NAHUM, THE POTTER

ʚ
ɞ

Years ago Nahum lived in the Golan. During the days of Joshua half of the tribe of Manasseh received a large holding of land on the east bank of the Jordan, for they (with Reuben and Gad) were primarily a shepherd tribe, and the elders reasoned that conquering pagan strongholds with flocks of sheep was not logistically efficient. For most of Israel's history those two and one-half tribes remained with their flocks apart from the real land of Israel.

Nahum would receive his father Ami-el's portion on the east bank upon the older man's death. But Nahum would inherit so much more than his father's small plot of land, for Ami-el was among the minority of Manasseh—he was not a shepherd. He was a potter for his tribe. A potter needs but little land to call his own—only his clay and his wheel. But everyone needs a potter.

From earliest childhood Nahum knew that he was born to be a potter. His soul had nothing of a shepherd in it. Ami-el was the potter of Golan, and someday Nahum would take his place . . . that was understood without question.

Now some would have resented such a destiny, but Nahum never did. His father had taught him that being a potter was a great and holy privilege. Shaping clay into a living form was as close to a divine act as Ami-el could imagine. Shaping clay was very much like the action of the Holy One (blessed be He) as He tenderly knelt by Eden's bank and kissed His children to life. It was a truth that the child Nahum had learned well.

From earliest childhood Nahum displayed unique ability with clay. Ami-el was himself a master potter, but he recog-

11

nized quickly his only son's talent. Young Nahum made the clay come to life. Not even Ami-el's own great skill could compare with his son's natural ability. With great pride he worked and prodded and praised his young boy to excellence. And those hours of teaching received ample reward.

His son's unique ability continually amazed Ami-el. While he was yet a young man Nahum began to produce miniatures on his wheel. The delicate pots and bowls and jars were perfect in every way. Joyfully the son would give them to his father as gifts for the children of the region. The little community became fascinated with the delicate miniatures and coveted them as much as they did the strong utilitarian pots and jars.

When Nahum was small the villagers would see the skilled potter leading his little boy out to the springs to show him the sources of the best clay. The father knew that someday he would turn this task completely over to Nahum so that he might more profitably spend his time at the potter's wheel. As you would expect, Ami-el was not one to use just any clay, and he taught young Nahum as a child that no one can accomplish any work of lasting quality with inferior material. Nahum learned well the sources of the perfect clay, just as Ami-el had known after his father had led him by the hand to the various springs. But quickly the day came that the father-teacher felt guilty at sending the boy after the materials. Ami-el protested that it was now Nahum who could better spend his time if the father himself gathered the clay and the young artisan only worked the wheel, but Nahum would not hear of it. He knew that his father was growing old, but he was still a master potter. "The young back will bear the burden," Nahum said, "and the wise old hands will still teach . . ."

While journeying to the clay beds Nahum had time to consider what would happen if he were to crush various minerals together. Could he perhaps find pigments that would render the clay a rich hue?

Would this make a style of pottery that would be all his own? It was from these first musings that Nahum developed a process that rendered his work absolutely unique from that of all other potters, even his venerable father.

When Ami-el grew too old for the wheel, he knew that his son was more than ready to carry on the sacred craft of pottery in Manasseh. He had ingrained Nahum well in the belief that there is nothing that is common. The shaping of the moist earth itself would continue in the young man's hands as a sacred obligation.

Ami-el lived to see Nahum marry Davra (a beautiful daughter of Sarah if there ever was one). The happy union produced two grandchildren, Itzak and Rahel. With such a legacy Ami-el knew that a man could go to his fathers in peace, and it was with both great sorrow and great honor that Nahum one day buried his mentor, his father.

Soon after Ami-el's death the Syrians began to stir. It had been more than 100 years since the last wars, and life during the land's period of rest had been good. But in a few short weeks all of that changed. The enemy bands penetrated farther to the south with each raid. All of the Golan was at risk. Since Israel had no standing army and there seemed to be no judge on the horizon to deliver them, the people of Manasseh began to flee the hillsides and look for refuge among the territories of their cousins across the river.

Davra and Nahum also fled before the invaders. Taking only the children and the pottery wheel, they left their homeland. The villages of the Jordan headwaters swelled with the refugees, and even those who lived in the region of Naphtali were uneasy at the possibility of Syria's approach. During any crisis hospitality comes in short supply, for the demand is great.

Finally Nahum brought his family to the Levite village of Kedesh. Entering the town, he began to search for the stalls of the merchants. It was his plan to offer his services to one of the shopkeepers in exchange for food and shelter for his family. They spurned his offer. There were already more refugees than the village could handle.

Finally Nahum met Azariah, the leather merchant. Azariah

was about to brush him aside when Nahum pulled a rough cloth from a pouch at his waist. As he unwound the fabric the merchant's eyes opened in amazement. The refugee held in his hand the most delicate miniature jar he had ever seen. As he took it and held it to the sunlight, it glistened with a fragile and liquid blue tint. Never had the man seen such artistry. The jar shimmered as living water in his hand.

Not wanting to appear too excited, Azariah hesitated before finally speaking. "This is a very interesting little piece of clay, my friend. How did you come to acquire this?"

"I made it," Nahum replied simply.

"I tell you I am a man of business, and I believe there might be a market for such work as this. I'll strike an agreement with you—if you produce pottery with such skill as this for me to sell, I will provide shelter and food for your family. Is this sufficient for you?"

Nahum was not in a position to bargain. Itzak and Rahel were tired from the journey. They needed to rest—needed a home. And that was how the master potter of Manasseh came to serve Azariah of Naphtali.

But Azariah was impatient. He wanted quick profits and had little time for Nahum to search the region for the quality of clay he needed. Daily Azariah would remind Nahum that up to that point the arrangement had been rather one-sided. Nahum would plead with the merchant to allow him the time to find the best materials, for then sales would be even more profitable, but Azariah was a shortsighted man.

It was with frustration that Nahum began to turn out the pots. It was only because of his great skill that the jars were the best in the territory despite the fact that the clay was inferior. Azariah listened to Nahum's protests each time he delivered a new batch to the market stalls, but he also reminded the potter that if it were not for his generosity Davra and the children would still be refugees. Nahum received only a fraction of the benefits that should have been due him, while Azariah made a handsome profit from the skills of his business "partner."

Nahum, the Potter

But Nahum's frustration was not at the arrangement itself but rather at the pressure upon him to produce less than he was dedicated to create. Destiny soon proved the relationship was not to last very long anyway, for the Syrians continued their progress through the northern regions, and soon even Kedesh itself was at risk. Quickly Azariah announced that he was going to establish himself near Jerusalem, and that Nahum would have to make his own livelihood again.

And so once more the potter of Manasseh found himself a refugee. The little family joined the fleeing villagers as they fled to the south before the invading enemy. Discouraged travelers skirted the western shore of the great lake and began the ascent up to the highlands of Ephraim. Nahum knew that again his only hope was to find a benefactor who would accept his service or his family was doomed.

After days of travel they came to the valley between Ebal and Gerizim. Only one place seemed to offer any hope in that area—the ancient town of Shechem.

Shechem had a long Jewish history. It was the site of Jacob's well and the area where Joshua and the elders laid the bones of Joseph to rest after so many years of exile in Egypt. The Hebrews confirmed the holy covenant with the promises of curses and blessings. But, at the moment, Shechem was also filled with the ragtag mass who had lost everything to the invasion.

Arriving at the east end of the village, Nahum looked for someone whose clothing indicated he was a citizen of Shechem. Quickly Nahum asked the first Shechemite he saw who was the most wealthy man in the region.

"You want a wealthy man? Ha, that is an easy question, my friend!" The Shechemite laughed as he replied, "There is none in all the hills of Ephraim, or maybe in Israel herself, so rich as Gedaliah. I am told he has a portion of the highway trade all the way to Egypt."

"And how," asked Nahum, "am I to find this Gedaliah?"

"That is easy. Just go past the main gate of the village, on beyond the well, and continue walking to the west. When you come

15

to the home of Gedaliah you will know it, I am certain of that."

Nahum led his family past the town to the far side of the valley. Suddenly there appeared before their weary gaze a manor such as they had never seen. A large wall surrounded a cluster of buildings. In the center rose a wonderful structure with gardens and decoration that seemed to have been created for a king. Never had the simple people of Manasseh even dreamed of such a place.

When Nahum reached the manor gate, a servant met him and demanded, "Do you have business in this place?"

"Yes, I do. I am Nahum, potter of Golan," he replied firmly.

"And does my master, Gedaliah, expect you today?"

"No, we have never met, but I would propose an arrangement with your master."

"I am sorry then," the servant replied kindly. "My master is a man of great importance, and many demand his time. It is my duty to protect him from distractions. Unless you can assure me that Master Gedaliah has business with you, I cannot allow you to bother him."

Nahum reached into his waist pouch and produced the cloth protecting the miniature pot. "Perhaps Master Gedaliah would be interested in a small token of my work and my sincerity." Nahum held the jar to the sunlight and allowed the light to flash off it through his fingers. The gatekeeper gasped at the stunning sight. Slowly he reached toward the vessel and gently took it.

The jar seemed alive, and the servant turned toward the great house without removing his eyes from the pottery. He was absolutely entranced by it as he carried it. Nahum turned to Davra and said, "I believe we have an appointment with Master Gedaliah."

In a few moments the servant returned again and said, "My master would be honored to meet with you, craftsman Nahum of Manasseh. Would you please bring your family and follow me?"

The family walked in amazement through the large courtyard. Servants went deliberately, but not with haste, about their appointed tasks. Even the least of them seemed perfectly content with their roles. When Davra and Nahum came to the door of the main room of the large house the servant assured them that the wheel would be well looked after and that they might enter to meet the master of the manor without concern for their few possessions.

Inside the door was a room of a size that the refugees had never seen before. It was not dark at all, but completely bright and open. This place was strange, for it seemed to be more than just a room, and hallways led off it to still other areas. Niches in the walls displayed objects of great beauty. Clearly Gedaliah was not only exceedingly prosperous, but also a man of impeccable taste.

Suddenly a dignified man appeared in a doorway. Without any trace of arrogance, he was imposing only in his dignity. The master's generous smile immediately put Nahum at ease when he spoke. "I am Gedaliah, and you my friend must be the potter of Manasseh, Nahum." Extending his arms in friendship, he led Nahum to a low table by the east wall where a small object sat alone. "Tell me, sir, are you truly the man who is able to create such a masterpiece as this?"

"Yes," Nahum replied. "The Holy One (blessed be He) has granted me the skill of my father, Ami-el, and more. I create these things to His glory and to the honor of my father (of blessed memory)."

"Well, master potter, I will not deceive you. Never have I seen such work as this. Only one who works under the influence of the divine Spirit could produce such beauty. I am honored that you would grace my home this day. But my faithful servant has said that you have a business proposition for me. Might I be so bold as to ask that we discuss your proposition over a meal this evening? Would you do me the honor of dining with me, and then we may discuss your mission this day?"

"Oh, Master Gedaliah, your generous offer is more than we can accept. We are but strangers and have nowhere to prepare ourselves in fitting manner for such an honor . . ."

But before Nahum could continue, Gedaliah called out, "Gershon, prepare a place for this good family. Please provide whatever they need so that tonight they dine with me." Immediately the servant appeared and led the family to a guest area. He even provided them fine clothing to take the place of their travel-worn garments.

And such a banquet it was. Gedaliah proved to be a more gracious host than they could have ever imagined. His wit and careful manner set all around him at ease. He was especially careful to include Itzak and Rahel in his conversation, and the children loved him immediately.

As everyone was reclining in comfort, Gedaliah broached the subject of Nahum's proposition. Nahum leaned forward intently as he spoke. "Master Gedaliah, I come to you as a stranger and a man who has no home. The land of my fathers was overrun by the uncircumcised, and we fled before them. We eventually went to Kedesh of Naphtali and hoped that an association with the merchant Azariah would be mutually a blessing, but he did not value my work as I wished. But soon that did not matter, as we all fled before the Syrians again. I come to you tonight to propose that I might serve you with my skill. All I ask in return is provision and shelter for my wife and my children. I promise that you will receive the very best of my efforts, and you may sell them for whatever price you can."

"Nahum, my good man, this would not be equitable. I would be taking incredible advantage of your magnificent skill! Never has there been one who can create what you do, and my wealth would be multiplied by your efforts. Nevertheless, I am not one to easily turn down a business proposition such as this. I have not prospered in this manner because I was a poor judge of opportunities. I will accept your offer. You will be granted refuge here in my home, and I will do all I can to assist you in your work. So let it be."

So the two men struck an agreement. Within days Gedaliah provided living space in the compound for the family from Golan. Nahum made a small work area by their new home, and he began to journey about the region of Ephraim hunting for clay. For days Nahum questioned the men of Shechem and followed leads about springs and streambeds. But each search brought disappointment, as he found only inferior clay beds. Each day he seemed to sense that soon Gedaliah might grow impatient with his searching. Yet the master was always gracious and only wished him good blessings in his effort.

Then one magnificent afternoon Nahum found his clay. It felt just like the clay of Golan and even smelled of Golan! He wrapped a large amount of it in a wet cloth and journeyed to Shechem. His heart rejoiced as he called out to Davra, "Feel it! Even the Lord Himself did not have better clay when He shaped Adam!" Davra laughed at her husband's childlike joy. The days of searching had accomplished one thing, for by that time Nahum also knew where to find the pigments he needed again to put his mark into his work.

It was with great joy that the potter of Manasseh presented his first vessel to Gedaliah. The master's hands held the piece with reverence, and the look on his face inspired Nahum to go back to work immediately. Soon the skilled hands of Gedaliah's new servant began to transform the clay into things of wondrous beauty.

Part II

NAHUM, THE POTTER

W ithin months the demand for the pottery of Gedaliah of Shechem grew until caravan masters passing by the well of Jacob paid top prices for every piece they could obtain. Rumor at the marketplace told that some of the bluish pottery went even to Babylon and Egypt. Cargo ships from Crete loaded the bowls and jars of Gedaliah to sell for magnificent prices throughout the Mediterranean. Some even whispered that they believed the vessels were now being used in Temple services at Jerusalem!

Soon Gedaliah expanded the living quarters of his most skilled servant. No longer did Nahum have to transport his own clay and other materials. He received workers of his own to bring it so that he might stay at the wheel as long as he wished. And the best part of the arrangement was that there was still time to create the miniatures that his master loved to give to the children of the area.

Nearly four years went by as Itzak developed skill on the pottery wheel himself, and little Rahel was promising soon to be a woman. One day Nahum was guiding his son at the wheel when a servant appeared at the entrance to the workplace. "Nahum, Master Gedaliah requests that tonight you and your family join him in dining," the man said.

Nahum thanked the messenger and announced to Itzak, "Today we put away the work early, for tonight we are graced to be with the master. Come, let us finish well."

By evening the family had prepared for the special honor of eating in the main house. As they approached it, Davra remarked about what a wonderful home this had been for them. The door opened and a servant bade them to enter. It had been a long time since he had been inside, and Nahum was stunned at what he saw as they entered. Many of the tables and display niches held jars and vessels and plates, each with a bluish hue. Assuming that the master had sold all his works, it had never occurred to Nahum that some of them were still there in the manor.

When Gedaliah entered the room, he announced, "Nahum, my friend, I am embarrassed for you to see this sign of my selfishness. There were times when you would create a piece and it was too beautiful simply to be sold. I could not part with what you had done. Do you remember any of these pieces?"

"I don't know if you will believe me, but I remember every one of them. They are as children to me at times," Nahum replied, almost blushing.

"Come," said the master, "let me show you something." He led Nahum to a small niche on the east wall. There, sitting on a finely woven cloth, was the miniature jar that had gained Nahum entry into the household nearly four years before. "Do you remember this little piece, my friend? This was your first gift to me, and I cherish it to this day."

Nahum choked back his emotion, and his host graciously delivered him from embarrassment by requesting that they all retire to the eating area. Again they ate slowly and with great joy.

When the meal wound down, Gedaliah spoke. "Nahum, four years ago you came to me and promised that you would bless me with your skills if I would but provide for you and for Davra and the children. Now Itzak is nearly a man, and little Rahel is the miniature of her mother. And I, I am enriched by your efforts more than I can tell. You have earned the name of Gedaliah respect and renown from Egypt to Mesopotamia. So now I would speak of a business proposition to you."

The master leaned forward intently as though he had been rehearsing his speech for some time. "I, Gedaliah, would now make up to you some of what I owe you. After this Sabbath the ram's horn will sound. The time of Jubilee has come. Release for all captives will be proclaimed. I plan to free you from your oath to me, but more than that—" from beneath his cloak Gedaliah produced a pouch and set it in front of Nahum as he continued, "more than that, I would send you away with just a portion of what you have given me. The bars of silver in this pouch are yours as I send you back to Golan. The Lord has delivered us from the hand of the Syrians, and it is fitting that you go back to live and to die in the land of Ami-el."

Gedaliah leaned back and smiled as he continued, "I will do more than this. I am giving you three servants of your own to assist you in your work. It is past time that the caravans should carry the pottery of Gedaliah. Let them from this day carry the magnificent works of the master Nahum of Golan!"

The gifts staggered Nahum, and he began to reply when Gedaliah held up his hand to silence him. "One thing more, my good friend. I have taken oath before the elders of Shechem that when I die one third of all I own is to go to you, Nahum of Golan, and to your children, as a legacy for the honorable service that you have given to me in my household."

Silence hung over the remains of the meal until Davra touched Nahum's arm. He knew what the touch meant. He then quietly said, "It shall not be so."

"What? How can this be? What are you saying?"

"No, Master Gedaliah, it shall not be so," he repeated. "Davra and I have talked long over this matter, for we knew well that the year of release was upon us. But we also know that we do not desire freedom from you. You have been our protector, and you have been our blessed father. Servitude in your house is better than freedom has ever been or could be.

"Gedaliah," he said with conviction, "we would become your slaves for life!"

The next morning a large crowd assembled at the gate of Shechem, for word had spread through the town that Gedaliah the merchant had requested a meeting of the elders. Speculation ran high as to what it might mean. One thing was guaranteed—if Gedaliah was formally meeting with the town elders, it would be an event that everyone would want to witness, for such an assembly meant that something solemn was to take place.

A whisper raced through the crowd as Davra, Nahum, and Gedaliah approached the gate. The elders waited for them as the merchant stepped forward. Gedaliah was not only the most prosperous man in the region but also the most magnanimous. Many in the crowd that day owed their livelihood to him. Others had received some kindness from his generous hand. He was universally loved and respected for his goodness.

It seemed that Gedaliah's presence was always dignified, but on this bright autumn morning he appeared particularly noble.

The crowd fell silent as Gedaliah began to speak. "Men of Shechem, hear me this day. Four years ago this good man, Nahum of Golan, came to my home as a refugee. The uncircumcised Syrian had driven him from the land of his fathers. As he left the hills of Manasseh he sought refuge in Kedesh of Naphtali, only to be mistreated by a trader there and then to be driven on by the Syrians again." The crowd well knew the story, for some of them had come to the hills of Ephraim in exactly the same manner.

"When this man appeared at my gate," Gedaliah continued, "he brought only his family, his potter's wheel, and his incredible gift. You know well of this man's skill and how he has the touch of Bezaleel and Aholiab." A murmur of agreement swept through the crowd, for the reputation of Nahum had become part of the pride of Shechem. "We struck covenant together that I would shelter him and keep him, and he would work his magic with clay for me. I have done my best to keep my part of the agreement, but there is no way I could equally repay my friend for what he has done for me."

Davra took Nahum's arm as he stood, almost embarrassed by such high praise from one so prominent.

"A few days ago I took counsel with you that my will might be known. Soon the shofar will sound and all that is bound shall be released. It has been fully my will that this good man should go back to the hills of his childhood not as one homeless, but as prosperous as befits his skill and dedication to his craft. I have offered him silver and three servants that he may reestablish himself in Manasseh." The crowd might have gasped at the amount of the gift if it had come from any other source, but they knew Gedaliah, and nothing of his generosity surprised them.

"More than this," the merchant continued, "I have told Nahum that I have made provision with you that when I die and am buried with our fathers he is to receive one third of all that I own, for he has become as a son to me." At that statement a loud stirring seized the assembly, for even Gedaliah himself could hardly be so magnanimous to a stranger in Ephraim. "It is true," he shouted above the crowd. "I have sworn such oath before the elders as witness!"

But then Gedaliah stunned the audience when he stated, "But it shall not be so. This man, my friend Nahum of Golan, has said this shall not be so. When I offered him my silver and my inheritance, he announced to me that he would rather be a life slave in my household."

The crowd exploded in surprise. This was an unexpected turn of events. Could it be that any man would reject such wealth and freedom?

A village elder stepped forward and raised his hands to bring the citizens to silence. When he finally had the attention of the crowd, the old man spoke with deliberate care. "Nahum of Manasseh, come here to me."

Nahum stepped forward directly in front of the village leaders and stood before them.

"Tell me, Nahum," the old man's steel-gray eyes pierced into the potter's as he asked, "is this truly your will? Do you, of your own accord and volition, with no coercion, intend this covenant?"

"I call you elders of Shechem to witness. I speak for Davra, my wife, and for myself, Nahum, son of Ami-el of Golan. I love my master and would seek slavery in his house before freedom until the day of my death."

Nahum turned to gesture toward his master and saw that tears filled Gedaliah's eyes.

Nahum, the Potter

"Quickly, then," the village patriarch commanded a young man standing near the gate, "fetch an awl and a mallet from the tanner's shop." In a moment the young man disappeared through the gate toward the area of the craftsmen's shops.

While he was gone the village elder took a small cloth from a pouch at his waist and held it by one corner so it fell toward the ground. Nahum understood the ancient sign of covenant. He reached out and took the lower end of the cloth in his right hand. Then the patriarch led Nahum by the cloth to where Gedaliah stood and extended it toward the merchant. Gedaliah reached for the corner held by the elder. Then the leader of Shechem took the middle of the cloth and led them both to the doorpost of the Shechem gate where the young man held the awl and mallet.

Nahum leaned against the gatepost and held his left ear against the ancient wood. The aged patriarch took the awl and with one swift blow drilled a hole through the potter's ear. As Nahum turned back to his master, Gedaliah took the cloth and held it to the bleeding ear and embraced his faithful servant.

Scarred for life, Nahum had marked himself in a way that would show all that never again could another own him. The master potter became forever the honored servant of Gedaliah, noble merchant of Shechem.

THE SHOFAR SOUNDS

During the days of Joshua's conquest, the division of the land occurred under the divine direction of the casting of lots. This apparently random process brought about an equity and logic that could have only been accomplished by Providence. As a result, to a great degree, it defused potential jealousies and territorial confrontations. With the exception of Ephraim's complaint, the partition took place without the potential jockeying that would be expected of normal human nature.

When the division concluded, the tribes with larger populations generally received larger segments of the land. Still, tribal numbers were not the only factor apparently involved in the Lord's thinking. The various tribes also seemed to receive areas of the country that best related to the needs of their general occupations. The shepherd tribes (Judah, Manasseh, Reuben, etc.) did not need nearly as much land. The divine lot accomplished that also.

God seemed to take into consideration one other factor in the final distribution. The Lord had told Israel that "wherever you put your feet it will be your land," and the children of the spies seemed to have the right to claim the territory their ancestors had particularly explored. We see this most significantly in the territorial claim Caleb and his heirs made.

The Levites, of course, received no land. They were to be sprinkled among the tribes so that they might be readily available to counsel and direct all Israel in worship. The 48 cities of the Levites spread the priesthood among the people.

Chief among the villages assigned to the priestly tribe were the six "cities of refuge." Located on both sides of the Jordan, they included cities in the north, in the central region, and the south. Numbers 35 shares God's purpose for them. Perhaps the story of Zaccai will share why those cities are important today.

Part I

THE SHOFAR
SOUNDS

•ৄ•

Zaccai lived joyfully on the homestead of his ancestors. The east bank territory of Reuben seemed perfectly suited for the shepherd tribes, and Mattan's son's flocks prospered and multiplied during the quiet years following the Exodus and Conquest.

His few journeys to the communities west of the Jordan taught Zaccai that except for the pilgrimage festivals to Shiloh, he had no need to leave his home territory. The memorial pillar erected by the fathers on the riverbank reminded all who lived in the east who they were and who their God was. That monument rendered the geographic separation from the other tribes as of little consequence. Zaccai did not miss his cousins because of his love for his pastoral home. He knew he was a part of Israel.

The shepherd looked forward to a long, full life with Zilpah and their boys. It would be his privilege to leave his blessed plot to four sons when he rested with his ancestors. Life in Reuben was good, and only one thing served as a continual irritation to Zaccai. Joram, the Gadite, was more than a neighbor—he was a challenge and a trial. Zaccai's flocks wandered the boundary between Reuben and Gad, as Joram's homestead edged up to the border region. Joram was a difficult man. It seemed that his only purpose in life was to steal other people's joy.

One week Zaccai might find some of the boundary markers disturbed, and he would confront Joram, only to receive abuse in return. Joram always offered some extended, lame argument about how his family had been disadvantaged by the original land distribution and that "it was about time the wrongs were corrected." Another week Zaccai would have to dispute Joram's claim to some young lambs that had strayed across the territorial line. Zaccai could not remember how many times he had requested a meeting between the elders of Gad and Reuben to mediate a dispute with Joram. They had argued about land, flocks, grazing rights, water rights, harvesting procedures . . . The list seemed endless. Joram, simply put, was an impossible neighbor.

Were it not for the neighbor life would have been wonderful and Zaccai, in a moment of frustration and stupidity, once made the mistake of expressing his feelings out loud. "If I could just get rid of that Gadite I would be an extremely blessed man," he rashly stated at an assembly. The day would come when that emotion would come back to haunt him terribly.

Late one spring Zaccai released his flocks from their protective pens, only to find that the small stream near the pens had shrunk to little more than a dribble. The dry season had not started yet, so it should not have dried up. Zaccai immediately suspected Joram. Somehow he knew the dry wadi was the handiwork of his neighbor from Gad. In frustration, Zaccai called for his eldest son, Nachman, and told him to take the flock immediately to a part of the valley where the stream would surely be unaffected.

Zaccai was angry. Joram was the one irritation of his life that could not be resolved. The Gadite had no excuse for his contrary nature. Years of frustration reached their climax as he quickly crossed the muddy streambed to face again his antagonist. As the shepherd walked, his pace quickened, and with each step, his rage built in him. The more angry he became, the faster he walked, which created a cadence that fueled the rhythm of his frustration to an even greater intensity. By the time Zaccai reached the brow of the last hill of his territory he was so enraged he was fairly running up the rocky slope. Never had he been so upset.

Standing atop the ridge, Zaccai stared down at the meandering stream in the valley. It was just as he had suspected, and his rage was justified. From the ridge Zaccai could see where Joram and a servant were placing large boulders to reroute the water.

As Zaccai stumbled down the slope, Joram glanced up and motioned quickly for his servant to leave. The young man scrambled up the bank on the far side, running toward the nearest Gadite village in the area. When Zaccai drew near he shouted in frustration, "Joram, how dare you do this thing?"

"And what business is it of yours, Zaccai? And what right have you to cross into my land? A man should be allowed to do his work on his own property without interference, shouldn't I?"

"You can't be that arrogant and oblivious!" Zaccai spit back. "You know this water flows through my pastures and that I water my flock with it until the dry season!"

"And why do you believe that is my concern?" Joram responded in anger. "The water here is my water. This is the water of Gad, the possession of my tribe, and you infringe on our rights with your presence. You have no right to claim anything on my property, and I want you off of my land!"

In his rage Zaccai began to shake. The Gadite's brutal insolence was more than he could comprehend. "Not so, Joram," he shouted, "not so! You know we have brought issues like this to the elders of our tribes many times before and always you have been rebuked, even by your own!"

Joram turned away in anger, and as he did his hand swung out and caught Zaccai's shoulder. Zaccai stumbled back and reached out, grabbing Joram's cloak as he lost his balance and fell. Joram took that reflex action to be an attack and turned upon Zaccai to defend himself.

In a matter of moments Zaccai stood over the rumpled form of his belligerent neighbor. Reality cleared his dazed mind as he saw the lifeless body. A small pool of blood slowly stained the boulder under Joram's neck. Joram was dead. Zaccai stood there for a moment, not remembering what had happened but knowing that his enemy was dead at his feet.

Hearing the clatter of pebbles, Zaccai glanced up to see Joram's servant disappear over the ridge, running toward the Gadite village. Immediately Zaccai began to panic, for he knew that servant would soon bring Joram's brothers, and they had every legal right to kill him on the spot without trial. The fact that the whole event was accidental was of no importance. Even the most unintended accidents could bring reprisal.

The shepherd's mind raced as he considered his only option. He had to get to one of the six Levite cities. The refuge villages were the only hope for someone who had accidentally killed another. God had designated six sites as havens for fugitives like Zaccai. They were spaced geographically in such a manner that a person could reach one in less than a day's journey. Once the slayer was inside the village perimeter no one could touch him without a fair trial.

He had to decide where to go. *Bezer is in our own Reubenite territory, but that is the first direction that Joram's family would expect me to run,* he thought. *No, I cannot go to Bezer . . . Golan of Manasseh is too far, and it's the other side of the Gadite lands . . . Gilead? No, Gilead will never do; it's in Joram's own tribal possessions. I need to try the west bank—yes, the west bank, that's it.* Zaccai's mind raced through his options. *Kedesh of Naphtali is several days' journey, and I might be caught if I tried to go that far. Shechem of Ephraim is in the highlands and an arduous journey from here . . .* Then the resolution seemed to quickly come to him. *Hebron, yes, that's it, Hebron of Judah. It's on a road I have previously traveled, and I may reach there in a day. . . .*

Even while he was still convincing himself that Hebron was the best solution for his dilemma, he was already running. Terror drove him toward the southwest along the boundary of his tribe. Everything inside of him yearned to turn toward his home, but he had no safety apart from the protection of the Levites. He ached for home. His anguished mind considered his wife and sons. Who would care for them? Who would explain his plight to them when the men of Gad crashed in looking for him? How could he bear leaving them with no explanation?

The morning sun continued to rise as the heat of the day and his panicked flight began to take their toll. The trees that lined the Jordan became visible in the distance as his parched tongue and burning lungs ached for relief. After several hours the exhausted refugee stumbled down the bank to the river. He didn't have time to look for a fording site, so the branches lashed at his face and robe as he thrashed into the muddy stream and floundered to its west bank. Dripping and haggard, Zaccai struggled up the bank to the southern river road, feeling as though he would collapse.

As the hours went by Zaccai sensed that he needed food or he would not be able to continue his flight much longer. He passed a barley field and took some of the ripening grain from along the edge. The law declared the fringe of all fields to be the property of the poor and needy. That day Zaccai had perfect right to harvest the edge. The grain allowed him to continue at a more measured pace into the late afternoon.

As the sun began to set, Zaccai wondered if he dare slow down, but he knew that he had expended nearly as much energy looking behind himself for the shadows of his pursuers as he had in his flight toward Hebron.

The path was clearly marked, for Israelite law required each man to dedicate a few days each year to repairing the roads to the cities of refuge. Zaccai knew well the section that led to Bezer near his land. Little had he known when he worked on it that one day he himself would desperately flee down one of the roads to safety.

Finally fatigue and wisdom overcame him, and Zaccai turned from the path to find a hidden cave where he might spend the night. The hard cave floor provided an ample spot to rest and a fair vantage point for observing the valley below. The exhausted shepherd scanned the horizon in the moonlight for any sign of pursuers. Eventually Zaccai stared at the heavens, and ached over the turn of events that had brought his world crashing down. The God of his fathers would now have to care for Zilpah and their sons. Zaccai could no longer bring them comfort. In fitful sleep he cursed his anger and struggled throughout the restless night.

Before the sun broke over the hills of Reuben he was again on the path ascending out of the valley. With aching legs and burning lungs Zaccai felt that he should not have stopped for those few hours during the night. He constantly thought he heard angry voices behind him, but then perhaps it was only the pounding of his heart in his ears.

By midmorning Zaccai saw Hebron in the distance. In any other circumstance he would have surveyed the town with wonder. Hebron held the tombs of Abraham and Sarah, Isaac and Rebekah, and Jacob and Leah. It was that village that mighty Caleb had claimed for his own before the conquest and was also eventually buried there. Hebron was a sacred spot to the Israelites. But on that day Zaccai's full effort and attention only focused on that 1,500 cubit ring of stones surrounding it. Outside the protected barrier he was in the territory of Judah and fair game for Joram's avengers. Inside the Levite boundary he would receive protection.

Just to the north he spotted a small cluster of Levite men working in the fields near the boundary. One of them looked up and saw the ragged Reubenite running agonizingly toward them. Residents of any of the six villages immediately understood such a sight. A tall, slender Levite dusted off his hands and robe and walked toward him.

Azariah arrived at the gate just as Zaccai collapsed inside the perimeter. Cradling the refugee's head, the Levite took a small waterskin and held it to the mouth of the exhausted man. "I am Azariah of Hebron," the Levite said calmly. "You are now safe from those who seek you. Rest here for a while and then I would be honored if you would grace my home this night."

Zaccai looked up into the man's kind face. In the eyes of the Levite the desperate man found only assurance and peace. Until the brothers of Joram came to bring their accusations Azariah would serve as sponsor and protector of the refugee from the hill country of Reuben.

Part II

THE SHOFAR SOUNDS

From the morning that Zaccai collapsed inside the protected zone of the Levites of Hebron, Azariah became Zaccai's anchor to security. Before they ever entered the gate of the village he was more than gracious to the shepherd of Reuben. Azariah's home became Zaccai's. The Levite family accepted him as one of them. Elisheva's mannerisms reminded him so much of Zilpah that he was stunned that they were not sisters. From that first evening meal Zaccai greatly appreciated the gentle care of his adopted family in Hebron.

In spite of their gracious hospitality, though, that first night was agony. How could the God of Abraham, Isaac, and Jacob reside in His heaven so seemingly unconcerned with the tragic plight of a simple shepherd? The stars over Judah looked just like those over Reuben. The night birds called with the same plaintive cry. Zaccai struggled with a larger world that seemed to continue though his smaller one had ended in a little valley on the border of Gad.

Zaccai did not want to be a burden on his Levite hosts. He knew that his life had centered around flocks and herds and his farming skills were limited. But he was determined to learn. The 1,500 cubit perimeter did not provide enough space to tend flocks and herds, so he helped in the nearby garden plots, and Azariah assured him that there was more than enough work to go around. Zaccai would have ample opportunity to grow in the life of the village. His lessons would begin that very morning.

Zaccai felt clumsy and ignorant but was determined to be an asset to Azariah's household and the Levite community that now protected him. Long lonely nights alternated with days of growing agricultural skill. After a few weeks Zaccai began to feel a bit more competent and useful. The pulse of Hebron seemed less alien and he handled his tools less awkwardly.

Late one morning, soon after the second full moon of Zaccai's life in Hebron, a small group from the village were working a field to the north of the village. Grape vines needed pruning and training. It was a strange new skill for the shepherd, but he was eager to learn. As the day wore on, one of the Levites noticed a band of travelers approaching Hebron from the road to the east. The garments of the six or eight men indicated they were from Gad.

One of the Gadites glanced toward the men working in the vineyard and cursed loudly. "I see you, I see you, Zaccai of Reuben! So you slipped into Judah to hide from your guilt. Well, your running has ended here, you viper! Now you will pay for the innocent blood of my brother Joram."

Others of the group echoed the shouts and threats as Zaccai stood silently. Azariah's strong hand reached out and touched Zaccai's shoulder as he spoke words of assurance. "Give them no concern at this time. We knew they would come, and now they are here. We must trust in the providence and wisdom of the elders of Hebron as they receive the accusations. It will surely be in the hands of the Divine One. Let us return to our work, for we have many wandering runners to deal with. Come, Zaccai, let us resume our labor."

Azariah's confidence again provided strength, and Zaccai felt overwhelmed with his debt to his Levite friend. The men went back to work. In a few minutes a messenger hurried from the village gate and announced, "Zaccai, son of Matthan of Reuben, the elders summon you to the gate to meet your accusers."

Zaccai glanced toward Azariah for strength. His friend smiled and said, "I will go with you." The Levite dusted off his robe and set his pruning knife down by the basket at his feet. "Come, my friend, we have known this moment would arrive. The Holy One will accomplish His will. He must. Let us go to the village."

The Judean Chronicles

The Gadites shifted and mumbled between themselves as Zaccai and Azariah approached the village. At least three of Joram's brothers stood in the cluster along with several other men whom Zaccai did not recognize. One of the men turned as they neared the gate, and Zaccai's heart sank as he looked into the angry face of Joram's servant. The young man had taken the story of the struggle to his master's family, and Zaccai was not certain exactly what tale he had carried.

Zedekiah, one of the aged and venerable elders of Hebron, called the assembly to silence. "Men of Hebron, men of Gad, hear me now. Today specific accusation is brought against Zaccai of Reuben by the kindred of Joram of Gad. We will now hear this matter, and then mercy demands that the judges weigh the evidence for at least one night before rendering a verdict upon the charge." The men of Hebron mumbled their agreement, for they had experienced the procedure of accusation before. Zedekiah continued, "And so now, Shimone of Gad, you, as the elder brother, may speak in this matter."

A middle-aged man stepped forward and cast an angry glance at Zaccai as he spoke. "Elders of Hebron, today my accusation is plain. This man, Zaccai of Reuben, did, with great malice, attack my brother Joram—and that without cause! He violently beat my brother. We found his body and bore the sad burden back to our home and to the burying ground of our fathers. This agony has broken our aged mother's heart, and none may console her in her loss. I thank the Holy One that our father, of blessed memory, did not live to witness this tragedy. This man's deed has shattered our family. No repayment will ever assuage our grief or fill our loss, but we come with the righteous demand that you fulfill your obligations under the sacred law and deliver this man to our hands that we may exact from him the punishment for his crime. He has taken our beloved and innocent brother from us without provocation—"

"Not so! Not so!" Zaccai interrupted.

Immediately one of the Hebron patriarchs cut Zaccai's protests short. "Silence! You will have ample opportunity to provide your testimony in this regard, but at this time we will hear from the men of Gad."

Zedekiah then turned to the accusers and asked, "Do you have witnesses? We know of your charge against this man, but do you have witnesses?"

"We do," Shimone said confidently. "We have Joram's own servant, Ephraim. He was there by the stream on that cursed morning."

The elder summoned the young man. "Ephraim of Gad . . ." The servant stepped forward. "What do you say in this regard?"

Ephraim cleared his throat, then exploded with anger and passion. "I was there. I saw him!" The young man pointed quickly toward Zaccai as he continued, "My master, Joram, and I were working together when we saw this man of Reuben approaching with a stone in his hand—"

"No! I had no stone!" Zaccai protested.

"Silence," ordered the chief elder. "You shall grant the accuser his rights! I bid you not to speak again until we call for your word in this matter."

Quietly Zaccai whispered to his friend Azariah, "No stone. I had no stone!"

Azariah looked firmly at him. "Trust, Zaccai. You must trust and speak no more."

His friend's strong rebuke discouraged Zaccai. Azariah seemed oblivious to his pain. Zaccai listened to Ephraim's false testimony and felt a growing hopelessness and panic. The world was crashing in upon him again, and there seemed no escape. The refuge of Hebron was slipping away with every word of Joram's servant. Zaccai barely heard the man's conclusion. "Yes, I saw him. He murdered my good master and then ran as a coward over the hill. I alone was left to bear the tragic message to the wife and family of my household."

The old Levite stepped forward and asked, "This, then, is your witness against this man? This you saw with your own eyes?"

Ephraim did not pause or hesitate as he spat out, "It is! That is the full truth of this matter."

Zaccai stared at his sandals. Slowly shaking his head in abject disbelief, he began to resign himself to his fate. Surely Ephraim's lies had sealed his fate. Heaven had abandoned the shepherd of Reuben. Why make him wait the agony of a night before they condemned him? Was that an act of mercy? He had no way to disprove Ephraim's story.

The old Levite spoke again. "Men of Gad, have you any other to testify against Zaccai?"

"Yes, yes," they echoed. "Much more," came the reply.

"Then let the next eyewitness step forward to speak," the elder proclaimed.

"I am Shemuel, near brother of Joram," stated a tall and dignified man as he came forward with confidence. "I have heard this man speak malice toward my brother and—"

"Hold now, Shemuel," one of the Hebron elders interrupted, "hold your peace. You have been asked for your witness of this event. Were you present at the death of your brother?"

"No, I was not," Shemuel answered, "but I well know the bitterness that this man held toward Joram for many years. I even know that he spoke what he would like to do to Joram—"

"Cease!" Zedekiah commanded with impatience as his old eyes flashed toward Shemuel. "The law is specific and plain. You will not speak of anything that you have not seen with your own eyes. If you were not present at the death of your brother, then you have nothing to say in this regard. We will not hear of your opinions!"

The aged Levite's voice rang with such authority that his presence and words silenced Zaccai's accusers. Slowly the patriarch scanned the crowd, then he broke the silence as he asked in measured tones, "Is there no other who witnessed this event? Is there no other who may say, 'I was there and I saw this,' as the servant has done?"

No one stepped forward. No one spoke. Zaccai waited for further condemnation, but it did not come. The Gadites shifted their weight and looked at each other in frustration. None could testify, for despite their solemn conviction, only

Ephraim could say, "This I saw with my eyes."

The Hebron fathers allowed further time for testimony, then nodded at each other knowingly. Finally, after an interminable silence, the eldest judge spoke calmly, "If there is no other witness, we shall render our verdict now."

"Now? Now?" Zaccai responded with shock. "What of my defense? Am I not allowed to speak in response to this servant's lies?" Zaccai looked at his friend Azariah in despair. "Azariah, help me, please!"

The chief judge abruptly reprimanded Zaccai. "Silence! You will hear our sentence."

Zaccai felt faint as his only hope vanished. His strength drained as the chief judge continued, "Our verdict is to be rendered upon the Law's demand. We have heard the testimony of the servant of the house of Joram. He has claimed an act of murder, but there is none to support his accusation. We don't know if Ephraim speaks the truth. Nor do we know if Zaccai is innocent of the charge. But the Law is clear. None may be condemned upon the testimony of a single person, and no one supports the witness of Ephraim. Therefore we proclaim Zaccai of Reuben to be innocent of this charge. He may remain under our protection. This is my pronouncement."

Joram's brothers began to protest angrily, but the elders silenced them. One of the Levites spoke over the shouting, "The Law is clear. Zaccai of Reuben will be harbored in Hebron. None may harm him without threat of judgment. This matter is now sealed in the Covenant Law!" The Levite judges then entered the city and ended the matter.

The Gadites snarled, "So you have escaped judgment for your crime?"

"Do not be arrogant, Zaccai. We know where you are!"

"If we catch you putting one sandal outside the perimeter of Hebron, you will justly pay for what you have done!"

The threats continued until a village leader returned from the gate to disperse the crowd and send the Gadites on their way. Azariah pulled Zaccai into the city to take him home.

From that day forward Hebron represented safety for the accused shepherd of Reuben. Outside the boundary lay condemnation—inside the line was protection. Zaccai was a free man within a 1,500 cubit world.

As time passed Zaccai became more and more ingrained into the pulse of Hebron. Month after month brought greater skill with farming tools.

When the three pilgrimage festivals rolled around each year Zaccai ached as most of the men left Hebron to visit the sanctuary which, at that time, resided at Shiloh. Each time the men would prepare to leave, Zaccai would ask his friends to inquire about the welfare of his family in Reuben. He loved Azariah and Elisheva and their children as his own, but his absence from Reuben was a constant aching within his heart. The breezes of Judah were never whispers of home.

Months rolled by and harvests and plantings followed each other. The cycles of the agricultural seasons and the rituals of everyday life filled his days, but Zaccai's nights brought emptiness. For nearly five years the man who had once freely roamed the hills of Reuben lived in a small restricted world. Within that circle Zaccai was a totally free man, but he never felt more than half a man. The other part dreamed at night of his home east of the Jordan with his growing sons.

Late one summer afternoon a runner approached Hebron from the north. He attracted little attention as he entered the village. A few moments later a man stood upon the wall and lifted the shofar to his lips. The distinctive sound of the ancient ram's horn drifted plaintively to the villagers. Something of great importance was to be shared, and people hurried quickly to the gate from all around Hebron.

As the crowd drew near, some speculated that the Philistines were threatening the land again, but others guessed that to be false, for the runner had come from the north and not the west or the south, as one would expect if the problem were from Philistia. Others countered that it could be a Midianite incursion. But the shofar could mean assembly, warning, a call to war or worship, so wiser heads urged patience and sought to defuse the wild rumors. Some agreed that it was pointless to speculate, since the elders would announce the news in a moment anyway. *Let us wait for Zedekiah. He will tell us* . . . seemed to be the thought that eventually prevailed as the older men spoke with a tone that implied that the discussion was ended. (Still a few of the young boys whispered in anticipation.)

When the whole community was fully assembled the crowd fell silent as Zedekiah mounted the parapet by the gate with the young messenger at his side. The old Levite lifted his hands to subdue the last few whispers. "Men of Hebron, hear me this day. I speak from a heart of great sorrow. Young Lemuel here, from Shiloh, has brought us exceedingly sad tidings . . ."

His voice broke, and the aged leader struggled to continue through his obvious pain. The whole assembly waited in silence except for the soft crying of Levi's young son Benanni, who was uncomfortable in the afternoon heat. The late sun radiated off of the wall as the people looked at the ancient robed man and tried to read the meaning of his anguished eyes. In the distance a village dog yapped while Zedekiah collected his measured words for the momentous announcement.

Finally the patriarch spoke again. "This day has Israel suffered a great loss. Eliahu, the high priest, has died and his son, Asaph, will now stand before the Holy One who lives behind the veil. . . ."

Eliahu had served for many years and had been universally revered for his strength and dedication. Everyone would miss his stable presence in the sanctuary.

For Zaccai the sadness of the announcement lasted for only a moment before he felt the strong hand of his friend Azariah upon his shoulder. Zaccai turned and saw the Levite's eyes as Azariah whispered, "My friend, you are now free to go home."

Of course! Of course! Zaccai thought. Israelite law declared that the refugee must remain within the safety of the Levite village throughout the life of the high priest. But upon his death those who had killed accidentally might go free and none could

41

harm them upon penalty of their own death.

Eliahu's death released him. Zaccai could go home!

That evening Zaccai tried to express his profound gratitude to Azariah and his wife, Elisheva, for their years of generous friendship and hospitality. But how could he share his sense of debt to those who had saved his life? A large segment of his life and memory would be forever rooted in the house of Azariah of Hebron.

The Levite couple expressed their appreciation for his assistance with their sons and the work that Zaccai had shared with them. They assured him that his hard work and friendship had amply repaid their hospitality. Azariah and Elisheva would truly miss their Reubenite brother.

Early the next morning, soon after the sun broke over the eastern hills, Zaccai bade farewell to his adopted family. Then turning from Azariah's home, he followed the narrow streets to the gate in the old wall. As he passed through it a flood of memories began to overwhelm him. Hebron had become a familiar world. For a moment Zaccai stood and recalled the desperate day when Ephraim had brought a false accusation against him and the terror he had felt. The words of Zedekiah echoed within him: "Zaccai now will be harbored in Hebron. None may harm him. . . . The matter is now sealed in Covenant Law."

Zaccai turned to walk through the fields where he had learned to farm. As he approached the boundary line he felt himself slowing. The thought of stepping outside it for the first time in almost five years was frightening. Until the day of Eliahu's death the world outside had been foreboding and forbidden. But this morning Zaccai was a free man.

The shepherd hurried toward the Jordan valley. With every breath his sense of freedom grew. None could now condemn him. He passed hills and wadis that he had not noticed through the tears of his previous journey.

Late in the day he approached the Jordan River in the valley, but now he had time to find a shallow ford. Nor did he have to glean from the fringes of the fields, for Elisheva had prepared provisions for his journey.

The shepherd crossed the glaring Jordan valley and began the climb up to the eastern highlands. Soon the sights and smells began to evoke warm emotions in his memory. Zaccai was again in the land of his fathers. He thought he should pause and rest but was much too excited as he reached the territory of Reuben. Night fell as Zaccai continued on in the moonlight. The stars were the same, but they appeared to be more the stars of Reuben than those of Judah that night.

By the time the promise of morning streaked the eastern sky Zaccai reached the summit of the last hill. His heart raced as he saw a strong young man going about his morning duties near the sheep pen. Zaccai's son was preparing for another shepherd's day.

BACK FROM THE DEAD

⁝

Christians often ask for advice on how to select a version of the Bible that will assist them in their study. Two primary concerns are readability and accuracy. Some Bibles are refreshing to read, but scholars have nightmares over how accurately they reflect the intention of the original text. Obviously the average layperson is at the mercy of those who have specialized education, and so they continue their search for something they can understand and trust.

Other texts have, at times, seemed to please some academics, but not everyone.

One will swear by the RSV,
Another stands upon the NASB.
What about this here NIV?

I don't want to be lost over the ABC,
"If King James was good enough for Paul,
It's good enough for me!"

In the mid-1980s a group of Jewish scholars ended the work of more than two decades when they completed the final installment of the *Tanakh*. English-speaking Bible students find themselves indebted to the Jewish Publication Society for this translation. The *Tanakh* is a visionary and courageous gift to Bible literature. It is the first common-language translation of the "Old" Testament done by Jewish scholars since the work of the "seventy" in Alexandria, Egypt, more than 200 years before Jesus. That historical work (called the Septuagint) has been the basis for much scriptural study during the past 2,000 years.

The *Tanakh* continues that heritage. It is lively, refreshing, insightful, and doesn't sound at all like a Christian text. The intentions and inflections of the three parts of the Hebrew scriptures—the Law (Torah=TA), the Prophets (Nevi'im=NA), and the Writings (Ketubbim=KH)—sing with new meaning to those who have no Hebrew abilities. The *Tanakh* is also faithful to the order of the original text, and it takes a while for King James Version Christians to find their way around in it. (Moses is where we expect, but Malachi is near the middle and the text ends with its logical chronological end of 2 Chronicles.)

An example of how refreshing the *Tanakh* is for study can be seen in the famous Messianic passage of the suffering servant in Isaiah 53. The Christian is used to hearing "We did esteem Him smitten, afflicted of God. . . ." The emendation of the *Tanakh* speaks of Him "as one who was leprous."

Micha, the tanner of Beth Zor, understood that text without translation.

Part I

BACK FROM
THE DEAD

⁝

Joses had taught his young son, Micha, that the work of a tanner was as sacred as that of a priest. Carpenters and farmers and potters and winemakers all had their role, but only tanners had the sacred responsibility of dealing with the remnants of something as sacred as life. "Never," Joses repeated again and again, "never are you to take lightly the privilege and sacred duty of your work! An innocent creature of the Almighty has died that you may bless the earth with its skin! If you cannot weep for its loss, you are not fit for the job. Wet the knife with your tears, my son."

The words sank deeply into young Micha's core, for he was, by nature, a sensitive person. When old Joses died and left the responsibilities of tanner for the region to his son the father's influence hung perceptibly in the little shop. Even the elders of the village sensed absolutely no change in the shop except for the absence of Joses' smile. Micha was his father's son.

Because the atmosphere of reverence permeated Micha's shop, people respected, even cherished, his work all the way to Jerusalem. It wasn't that there were no other tanners available to mend a harness or repair a wineskin, it was just known by the faithful that the tanner of Beth Zor would do his work honorably and with dispatch. Many people appreciated the kind and gentle spirit of the young man who handled the skins and preserved the leathers. To Micha, his tanner's shop was a sacred place.

Of all the work a tanner would perform, one task Micha held in highest regard. It was one thing to take the gift of a living creature to create a sandal or pouch, but it was another level of sacredness to use the skin for making parchment for Torah.

Back From the Dead

On the days when Micha would turn his attention to the needs of the scribes and teachers, he did so with a gentle reverence. As his gifted hands would slowly scrape and treat the skin, he knew that soon a trained scribe would be copying, one sacred letter at a time, the Holy Word. When he came to any blemish, stain, or apparent imperfection in such a skin, he judged it very carefully, for he was constantly aware that on that very spot the scribe might write the name of God. If his keen eye could see no hope of correcting that weakness in the material, he would reject, with sorrow, the gift of the innocent lamb.

Because Micha was so conscientious, the Temple scribes came to treasure his products most highly. They knew that when they received a delivery of parchment from Beth Zor they could proceed with their sacred work without any fear of losing weeks of effort to a blemish that lesser tanners would ignore.

Many Israelites held the work of the tanner in low esteem. The stench of the tanning process, the continual dilemma of ritual impurity because of contact with dead animals, and the crude nature of some tanners offended them.

Because of this the scribes of the second Temple period even allowed the wives of a tanner to divorce their husbands, an option other wives did not have. All the wife of a tanner had to say to get a divorce was, "I thought I could live with his profession, but I can't." No one would blame her if she asked for a divorce.

Villages might force the tanner to live downwind from them.

But Micha's gentle nature and sacred attitude earned him esteem in the community of Beth Zor and the surrounding region. Thus he was an anomaly—a man well respected in a profession that most looked down on, even though it was a vital social role. To be considerate of his neighbors Micha did the tanning away from the village. He only stitched and smoothed the leather in the little shop adjacent to his home.

Esther, his wife, felt uniquely blessed to be married to a man of such conviction and reputation. A warm security filled the simple home in Beth Zor as she nursed her new son, Nattan. Someday little Nattan would toddle into the shop of Micha and also learn the "sacred work" of the tanner. She softly sang psalm-lullabies about the Temple, and Abraham, and Torah to her baby as she heard Micha working in the room adjacent to their home. This was as rich a life as a daughter of Sarah could desire, Esther believed.

One day as Micha was stitching a particularly strong harness for his old friend Matthias he glanced at the back of a knuckle on his left hand. A small bump seemed to be rising from the flesh. It did not hurt at all when he scraped at it with his fingernail, so Micha dismissed it.

"Everyone has little bumps and imperfections," he thought. "Besides, I probably scraped myself with one of the tools a few days ago. It happens all the time to a man who works with his hands."

Micha felt somewhat more curious a few days later when he was bouncing young Nattan on his knee just before they put the child to bed for the night. The young father noticed that not only had the spot not receded, but if anything it had increased a bit in size and was joined by another small bump farther down the finger. That still was not much of a concern to a man who had cut his hands many times in his labor. He put it out of his mind as he handed the happy boy to his mother. Still, as he stroked Nattan's hair as the child slept later that night, he noticed that the blemishes seemed more pronounced.

A few days later, soon after rising, Micha borrowed Esther's bronze mirror after he washed the sleep from his face. There seemed to be a slight scaly patch just off the tip of his nose and another just above his left eyebrow. A distant sense of foreboding began to grow within him. It appeared that something might be wrong. Later that day Esther made a brief comment about the spots, but her husband laughed and embraced his wife, teasing her about how she must be losing her love for him when she began to look for blemishes. Esther returned his jesting by stating that she had truly fallen for a younger man and that at that moment he was fussing for attention. She turned from Micha with a laugh and he smiled, but felt a growing uneasiness deep in his soul.

Back From the Dead

As the weeks passed he found more unexplained patches. Esther mentioned them no more. A certain universal defense mechanism lurks in the human heart. It seems that if we refuse to say something out loud we believe it may go away. Esther knew the dark word that haunted her nights, but she would not speak it.

Micha also knew the word that nibbled at the edges of her thoughts, but he played the game as well. Soon he began to notice that he was turning himself slightly away from people during conversation. When he would receive payment for his work he, at first, would pull down his sleeves to hide his hands a bit. In a few weeks he found himself asking his customers to just set the payment on the bench while he continued his work. But the patches of skin soon became too obvious for even that.

One day Johanen came to the shop. A respected elder in the region, he had been a close friend of Micha's father, Joses, for many years. Johanen came to the doorway, brushed his fingers to his lips, and then touched the sacred mezuzah on the doorpost. The patriarch then cleared his throat. "Ahem, good day to you, young Micha."

"And good day to you, honored Johanen. And how is the friend of my father (of blessed memory) this day?"

"I am well, my son. I am well. But this day I am not concerned for myself," the old man replied.

"I am pleased to hear you are well," Micha said as he stood up from his bench. "But I fear I sense frustration in your voice. It is not the wineskins that I repaired for you I trust. If there is a problem with any of them, I will make it right for you. I have no fear that they can be mended, for they were of good leather and should yet have many harvests in them."

"No, no, Micha. I am not concerned for the wineskins. The wineskins are in excellent condition and you repaired them masterfully, just as your father would have done."

Micha scowled a bit and asked, "Then what could your concern be of? You seem distressed."

The older man shifted his weight deliberately and then slowly took two steps forward as he said, "Yes, I am concerned.

49

I am concerned for the son of Joses." The silence hung above the stench of tanning skins. "I am concerned that the son of my dear friend has forgotten his obligations under the law."

Micha knew. For days the Torah demand had been growing within his heart. "When there is a rising of the skin, a white blemish, let that person who has such blemish show himself to the priest. . . ." But Micha could not bring himself to face the matter. He also knew, just as he had known for the weeks that the patches had been increasing, that one morning he would wake up and the roughness would be gone. He did not need to be examined by a priest—surely the spots meant nothing.

But in his deepest heart Micha realized differently.

Johanen interrupted his thoughts. "Micha, my son, have you shown yourself to the priest?"

"No, I have no need. I am quite sure that this means nothing."

"Oh, with all my heart I pray that is so," the old man continued, his eyes glistening. "I only know that the village is beginning to whisper about this matter, and the law is clear, my son. You have no choice. You must show yourself to the priest!"

"Johanen, I know you mean well, but again I assure you it is nothing."

"In the sacred memory of your father, again I say I pray that you are right, but there is no option under the law for you." Johanen leaned forward to touch his friend's shoulder, then was horrified when he saw his own hand pause for a moment and drop before it touched the young man. "I would give my life for yours, and for the grandson of Joses any day. But my prayers do not change the demands of the sacred law. I urge you, Micha, I urge to see the priest immediately. Our best hope is that you will be proclaimed clean and all this shadow lifted from our lives."

Micha, hurt and scared by the evident failure of Johanen's ability to touch him, finally replied, "For you, old friend, for you I will go to Temple."

Late that night, as Esther was nursing their young son, Micha said casually, "Tomorrow I go to the Temple. I have some parchments to deliver to the scribes in the court of the Sanhedrin. I shall not be long, for I have very little business beyond that."

Esther bit her lip. She knew what he was really going to the Temple for. But she could not say the terrifying word out loud.

When the baby was asleep, Esther busied herself rolling out her own sleeping mat, and Micha stared out of the doorway at the patch of sky over the courtyard. God's stars were there, but it seemed as though God Himself had left the heavens.

In the morning Micha seemed to dawdle around the little home, and it made Esther nervous, for her young husband was a conscientious man. Wasting time seemed so unlike him. Finally, as the midmorning sun warmed the clean walls of the home, Micha said, "Well, I suppose I will hurry on to Jerusalem now. I should not be long, for I don't have much serious business after I deliver the parchment."

The young man brushed out the door just as Esther was turning to bid him farewell. Tears fell upon the baby as she changed him that morning.

Normally Micha rejoiced at every opportunity that he had to go to the Temple. In his simple heart he held the deep conviction that God still dwelt on that Temple mount despite the obvious excesses and intrigues of the priestly class.

The building itself was marvelous. The Temple, its courtyards, and the surrounding colonnades dominated the man-made platform between the Valley of the Cheesemakers and the Kidron.

More than 400 years before, the returning exiles under Ezra and Nehemiah had reestablished the sanctity of the site after the Babylonians and many corrupt kings had desecrated the shrine. Herod the Great, genius builder and corrupt tyrant, had massively expanded the Temple in a vain attempt to gain the loyalty of the Jewish people. He constructed retaining walls to support a platform so that the slope of Moriah could be flattened out toward the south and the west. Over that southerly wall the Court of the Sanhedrin met in one of the colonnaded buildings along the edge of the Temple mount. The plateau of the Temple mount itself was paved in stone (mostly marble).

The Judean Chronicles

Four courtyards led to the Temple itself. The largest of them was The Court of the Gentiles. Anyone could enter it, and many "God-fearers"—Gentiles attracted to Judaism but who had not yet converted—would meet and mingle there. Beyond the gates was a smaller rectangular court for Jewish women. A smaller courtyard was reserved for only Jewish men. Finally, inside The Court of Jewish Men, gates led to The Court of the Priests. That last, exclusive court served as the courtyard for the Temple structure itself.

Micha, as did all faithful Jews, thrilled at the sight of the Temple. Surely there was no more grand building on earth. (Even a Roman general proclaimed it to be so as he passed through Jerusalem one time.)

But on that day Micha's steps were slow and deliberate, for the Temple stood not as a sign of the Holy Presence to one blemished, but rather it was the monument of potential condemnation. Because of his unsteady pace it was midafternoon before the Temple came into view. The tanner approached from the south as always, but instead of entering the Hinnom (Dung) Gate, as was his usual practice when he was going to the administrative end of the Temple, now he turned to the east and rested on the slope of the Mount of Olives for a while. Micha prayed as he faced the building his people had erected for their God to dwell in. The tanner was not so sure that He resided there anymore.

Eventually he realized that he must hurry into the Temple or the doors would be closing soon, for the sun showed that the time of the evening sacrifice was drawing near. Micha picked up his bundle of parchment and delivered them without ceremony to the storehouse of the scribes. At that point he was seriously tempted to just hurry home to Esther and Nattan. He desperately wanted to believe that he would wake up from his nightmare, but the words of Johanen rang in his ears: "You must show yourself to the priest. . . ."

After pacing and stalling as long as he was able to in the Court of the Gentiles, the tanner from Beth Zor worked his way through the exiting women at the gate toward the Court of the Men. A priest approached him. "I'm sorry, sir, but the Temple will be closing, since the evening sacrifice has been completed and the gates are soon to shut."

"Oh, I'm sorry, but I need only a few moments. You see, I am only here at the urging of an old friend. He's a bit concerned for a little problem that I have . . . I'm sure it is nothing . . ." Micha stumbled for words.

"A problem?" The priest looked intently at the young man. "Oh yes, I understand. There is a small problem here. Come with me, won't you please?" They passed through the Court of Men to a small side room at the edge of the priestly courtyard. When they arrived in the room Micha did not notice much of the interior—he just felt a growing despair from the reality that was deep inside him.

The priest took a torch from a bracket on the wall and held it near Micha's hands and face. As he began to inspect the patches of unusual skin, he spoke assuringly. "My name is Shemai. I am pleased to have the opportunity to assist you. I do hope, with all my heart, that I will soon have you on your way home. And what is your name?"

"I am Micha, son of Joses of Beth Zor. I am a tanner."

"Micha, a tanner . . . Oh yes, you provide us with some of the finest leather and parchment. Your work is highly respected . . ." The priest's voice dropped as he looked more closely at the blemishes. Micha's breathing was shallow and rapid, and all he could hear was his heart racing inside him.

Finally Shemai spoke again. "I'm sorry, Micha, I must ask that you return in another week. I will pray for you, and I do trust that we will see improvement in this condition, but you must appear before me again in seven days."

It was the last thing that Micha wanted to hear. He had dreamed that the priest would tell him, "I know you must have worried about this, but your fears had no foundation. This is a very common condition and means nothing. . . ."

But to see the priest again in a week meant that he was concerned and trying not to be in a hurry to condemn. Micha mindlessly mumbled his gratitude and went blindly out through the various gates until he found himself, quite by accident, in the center of the city. The young man finally came to his senses, found his bearings, and headed down the south road past Bethlehem.

It was quite dark by the time he approached his childhood village. Micha paused for a moment outside his home to lean his head toward the old mezuzah on the right doorpost. He yearned for relief from the burden that was growing inside of him. The young father tried to be pleasant when Esther spoke of her concern for his late arrival. They made small talk as she prepared the baby for bed, and then Micha acted as though he did not notice the tears as his wife combed out her hair. He told her he needed to move something in the little work area adjacent to the home, and taking one of the small oil lamps, retreated into his little refuge. The tanner reached for a broken harness, idly twisted the fresh leather patch, and began to cry.

The next six days were agony. The young couple lived each day and night in a fearful silence. Micha did his best to stay as busy as possible, but he would often find himself staring at his hands. Scraping softly at the dying flesh with his tools, horrified that it did not seem to cause him pain, he wondered how anything that shattered the heart so deeply could be so painless.

The young husband began to notice that Esther often sat staring blankly at the wall. Even Nattan's whimpering would often not stir her to reality. It was as though death had already passed through the little home of Beth Zor.

On the seventh day Micha concocted a weak excuse for leaving for the morning, and Esther held her tears until he was out of sight, heading north toward Jerusalem. She knew that a priest was waiting at the Temple for her young husband.

The painful journey to Jerusalem seemed, if anything, longer than the previous trip. Micha was absolutely oblivious to the fact that the roads to the city were more crowded than usual, for the pilgrims were beginning to swell the highways in preparation for the Passover celebration. His thoughts recently had been totally absorbed by little white patches and nightmares. (In fact, he had been surprised the previous day when he overheard two friends from Beth Zor discussing their plans for Passover that year.) His only thought was an overwhelming, aching desire for the angel of death to leave his home, depart from his body. But the angel seemed to hover over everything. During the long nights he felt the brooding presence of its wings.

Micha tried to slip unobtrusively into the inner courts of the Temple structure. He stood beside a pillar on the north side until he spotted the priest, Shemai, concluding the sacrifice procedure with a worshiper. Then he watched as the penitent sinner (whose dress indicated him as a pilgrim who had traveled from a great distance) left the gate. The joy on the faithful man's face was obvious. Apparently that Jew had fulfilled the dream of a lifetime, having come to worship his God in the house of his God. Micha yearned to share that sense of acceptance.

Shemai turned from washing at the great laver and looked around. As if providence had ordained it, the priest's eyes met Micha's. Without a word between them Shemai gestured for Micha to follow him to the side room again. Once inside the room, the priest spoke encouragingly as he again slowly inspected the blemished areas. Micha did not really hear what Shemai said. A growing numbness had taken over his mind just as surely as it was spreading throughout his body.

Finally the silence brought the tanner to reality. "What was that? What did you say?" Micha asked the priest.

"I said, I am sorry, but I must ask you to return to see me again in seven days."

The words echoed in Micha's throbbing mind all the way back to Beth Zor. When he found himself leaning up against the doorpost, the habit of a lifetime took over his actions. He realized that he had tilted his head to show deference to the parchment in the mezuzah just as naturally as one foot had fallen in front of the other all the way home from Jerusalem.

What did the parchment say? *"Schma, Israel, Elohim yireh . . ."* *("Hear, O Israel, the Lord is your Lord . . .").*

Micha ached to know where that God was. The God of Abraham, Isaac, Jacob, and Joses seemed to have forsaken the faithful tanner of Beth Zor.

Seven more agonizing days passed in the little home. Esther tried her best to maintain courage, but the husband she had known had already died. The empty shell of her husband held her son, and even that body was deteriorating. The young couple spoke little. The night hours they spent in silent tears, and daylight brought no reprieve from the agony of the darkness.

Finally the agonizing week ended. The death angel's breath seemed to fill the little home until the young couple arose to the choking reality of the last day. It was a dismal morning that brought a late spring rain. Without the early sunshine the home seemed particularly dark. Micha thought the weather was appropriate for such a day. A bright sun would have mocked his aching heart. Quietly, he told his wife, "I go to Jerusalem today."

"I will go with you," Esther replied, her eyes brimming with tears. "The baby will spend the day with my sister, Hannah."

He did not have the strength left in him to argue with her.

Micha was in agony as they went by Hannah's home. He wanted so much to hold his son one last time. Looking at the tiny hands, he knew that he would never guide them in the sacred skills of the tanner, as his father Joses had guided his. But he could not bring himself to touch the innocent child. Little Nattan's skin was so perfect. . . .

As the couple turned to the north alone, Esther, without speaking, reached out and took the arm of her husband. Instantly Micha resisted, but the scared girl hung on and would not let him pull away. The young husband quickly relented and the sad spectacle continued all the way to Jerusalem. They were not much more than children themselves. Micha was trying to give her strength, and Esther was struggling to be strong for her once handsome husband. The two crumbling pillars were doing their best to support each other on the dismal path to condemnation.

Back From the Dead

Eventually they reached the Temple mount and slowly ascended the eastern steps to the Golden Gate. The courtyards were less crowded than usual, for the rain had kept away many people that morning. As the young couple from Beth Zor approached the portal that separated the Court of Women from the place of Jewish men two priests stood waiting. One was Shemai, and it was evident that the other was waiting to escort Esther to a site somewhat out of the way. With some effort Micha pulled from her grasp to follow Shemai to the inner sanctum.

Shemai motioned for two other priests to join him, and the four men went into the room. Once inside, each of the three slowly, carefully studied Micha's hands and arms and face. They held the torch close as they inspected him. Its heat was uncomfortable. The men remained silent until each finally stood back and then went to a large basin to bathe himself. Wordlessly the two other priests undressed and put their robes onto a pole that would carry them to the altar for burning. Micha was afraid of what it meant. He sensed that in a few minutes Shemai would do the same thing.

Then Shemai stepped forward and sadly pronounced, "I am sorry. I do this day proclaim you unclean. From this time forward anything you touch shall be rendered unclean. You shall isolate yourself from society, for even the air you breathe will be tainted of death." The priest raised his hands painfully and slowly as he finally said, "Micha, son of Joses, I proclaim you leper. . . ."

The once virile young tanner of Beth Zor moaned aloud as the door opened to the courtyard. He finally crossed to the doorway and lifted his hands in agony, groaning, "I am a dead man! I am a dead man!"

From the side of the court Esther suddenly tried to break free so that she might run to embrace her husband, but the priest restrained her, and she collapsed on the marble pavement, sobbing. From that dismal morning on death reigned in the little family of Beth Zor.

Part II

BACK FROM THE DEAD

Micha's journey from the Temple precincts that rainy day led him northeast of the city toward the Judean wilderness. That desolate land had sheltered areas and caves where others who had come under the terrible finger of God found slim consolation among the fellowship of the cursed. One village not too far from Jerusalem was inhabited by lepers. Sometimes generous individuals would leave the city, heading up into the Galilee or following the Damascus road through ancient Jericho, and carry extra provisions for the living dead. Generally people encouraged the relatives of the lepers to accept the fate of their loved ones, and to begin to count their day of death from the time that the priest sent them out of the Temple, condemned. The pronouncement was a final one. Only strangers would care for the corpses that still walked and breathed in the valleys and settlements of the lepers.

Some lepers would cling to life for years. Others seemed blessed in that they died much more quickly and did not suffer as long. Micha was one of the "blessed" ones. In a matter of months he could tell easily the progress of his decline. Each passing season brought more evidence of the accelerating destruction of his body. Daily Micha was dying, a small piece at time.

Micha discovered by the second spring that the sense of feeling in his extremities had almost vanished. It was most evident when another leper asked him to help move a stone beneath which they had stored a small but treasured cache of food. Micha heard his fingers snap as he struggled with the boulder. He had unknowingly put too much pressure on them. Later that year, in the early autumn, he was horrified when he awakened one night to the nauseating smell of burning flesh. The former tanner of Beth Zor had rolled over into the remnants of his little fire.

But it was fall and the month of Tishri brought the pilgrims to Jerusalem to celebrate Sukkoth. Thousands of the faithful journeyed from all over the empire to return to Jerusalem for the memorial of the wilderness dwellings. The lepers were, of course, excluded and never allowed inside the city wall. But even in the village of the dead, rumors and whispers flew that year. It seemed that an itinerant prophet from the Galilee was performing wondrous deeds. The whispered news was that He had shown Himself capable of healing blindness and injuries and diseases of many kinds.

Some of the lepers wondered about the tales, but refused to consider the possibility that the man from Nazareth might be the new Elijah. If that was true, then perhaps even a half a man who lived among the lepers might have hope. But a disease that eats at you from the inside out also consumes your hope. Those who did discuss the rumors about Jesus carefully avoided raising the issue of leprosy because it was God's curse, and no one had cured a leper in more than 600 years. Many doubted that anyone could do it again, while some even dared to suggest that it had never happened in the first place, for it was only part of the myth and legend of a God who once parted seas and made a nation out of Egypt's slaves.

Micha wondered. At night he yearned for Esther and Nattan. His mind ached for the feel of leather and tools and parchments while what was left of his fingers could not. He could never quite resign himself to surrendering his God. God had surely abandoned him, but the faith of Joses ran deep in the simple man of Beth Zor. The rumors of a living prophet seemed to keep what was left of him alive.

One day, soon after Sukkoth had passed, Micha knew that he must seek out Jesus without any delay. He realized that he might not survive until the next spring when the Passover would bring the faithful again to Jerusalem. If Jesus would not pass by again he would perish. Micha left the colony of the hopeless.

For several days the ragged leper struggled along the edges of the road to the north. His progress would have been slow enough because of his condition, but he was delayed even more because he knew he must remain on the fringes of the road to avoid the other travelers. Usually he did his best to remain completely out of sight. If any did see him they responded in terror.

Late one morning Micha knew by the landscape that he must be approaching the southern shore of the Sea of Galilee. At that point he realized that he would have to receive some help or he might never locate the man Jesus. Eventually he found a clump of low brush along the main north-south road in which to hide himself. In a few minutes he heard a small group heading toward the lake. When the travelers were close enough to hear him, Micha called out, "Strangers, for the mercy of the Almighty, have you heard of Jesus of Nazareth?"

One of the men peered toward the bush and answered in astonishment, "Why yes, I have. Do you seek Him?"

"Yes, kind stranger; can you tell me where He is?"

"Of course, but more than that, you may travel with us if you choose. I have heard that He was staying in the home of the son of Jonas of Capernaum but has recently journeyed to the east side of the lake. We intend to take the juncture on the road to skirt the south side and head toward Bethsaida, where we have business. Come, join us for the companionship . . ."

The traveler stepped toward the bush as if to assist Micha, and Micha cried out, "No, you must stop! I may not travel with you, kind stranger. Please, be gone," he implored.

The group of men looked surprised but shrugged and began to head up the path. *Bethsaida,* the leper thought, *I know of that village. Perhaps I may reach there by tomorrow.*

Early the next morning as the sun rose to his right it seemed to set the hills on the western shore on fire. Micha rested for a few moments and looked down from the brow of the hill that he had been struggling up. The reflection of the hills was beautiful on the lake. The fishermen of the lake were just returning with the catch of the night, and Micha wondered if the morning would introduce a new day of hope or if his journey would bring only rejection and failure.

As the leper struggled to stand and continue on his way, he noticed a band of women on the path below him as it skirted the shoreline. They appeared to be from Bethsaida and heading to the lake. Some would clean fish, others would do laundry, while still others were just preparing to carry water to their village homes. Silhouetted by the sunrise, Micha shouted from the ridge of the hill, "Daughters of Galilee, do you know of Jesus of Nazareth? Is He in your village?"

Several women turned, shading their eyes as they stared up at the man in the sunlight. Finally one of them replied, "Jesus? The prophet? No, He has not been in Bethsaida for quite a while."

Micha's heart sank. How was he ever to find a prophet who seemed to have no home? Finally he called out desperately, "Do any of you know where He might be now?"

One of the younger women replied timidly, "I have heard He has gone to Jericho."

"Jericho?" cried the broken man, "Jericho?"

"I cannot say for sure," the young one added. "It is just what I have heard from the talk around the lake."

Micha's shoulders sagged in the morning sun as he slowly turned back south. By late afternoon he was exhausted. What was left of his feet was bleeding. His head throbbed from the sun's constant glare. Even the birds of the lake region seemed to mock him from the merciless sky. Returning down the shoreline took longer, for his steps were sporadic and stumbling. The dying leper knew that his journey would soon end. He would either fall at the feet of the prophet or die on a lonely path somewhere off the main roads of the Galilee.

Toward evening he spotted a small caravan at the crossroads on the south end of the lake. The merchants appeared to be on their way to Jerusalem with produce from the highlands on the north shore. In desperation Micha hurried to a large boulder and awaited their approach. Finally as they neared his hiding place and he feared he could remain hidden no longer, the leper called out, "Men of Israel, in the Name of the merciful, I beseech you. Have you seen the one called Jesus who is from Nazareth?"

The five men brought their donkeys to an abrupt halt. Suspicious, they began to scan the landscape around them nervously.

"Please," Micha cried, "please, have you seen the prophet from Nazareth named Jesus?"

The man who appeared to be the leader of the band commanded, "Show yourself! I will not stop to talk to a rock!"

The leper appealed in tears, "In the mercy of David, all I ask is that you tell me of Jesus."

"Step forth that I may see who I am facing or we will . . ."

The caravan fell back as they saw the man stumble from behind the boulder. One of them looked as though he was going to be ill. A half-decomposed man was not what they expected. "Be gone from us," they screamed. "Away with you!" And they picked up stones and began to hurl them toward Micha.

Micha collapsed as one of the stones struck his shoulder. He screamed (more to heaven than to the men of the caravan), "I beg of you, please tell me where to find Jesus!"

At the pitiful sight of the fallen man the horrified merchants paused. Still they retreated slightly as one of them shouted, "He is in Capernaum. We saw Him there just today. Now be gone with you," and he picked up another stone to threaten the helpless leper.

Micha staggered to his feet and forced his battered and diseased body to struggle back into the ravine by the roadway. He heard the caravan hurry off down the road, and when it appeared that they would be no threat to him any longer, the leper stumbled to the place where the lake came right to the road juncture. After a few minutes of washing his wounds and drinking from the small pools between the boulders along the shore, Micha determined to again head north, but this time he would follow the western shoreline and pray that his strength would last until he got to Capernaum.

Back From the Dead

Several times during the night the battered man collapsed by the side of the road in a fitful slumber. When he awoke he again struggled on in the bright moonlight down the empty path. The coolness of the evening turned clammy as the dew began to dampen his clothes. The leper shivered in the early-morning hours but realized that the cover of darkness had allowed him to make better progress, since the road was empty at night. It had enabled him to skirt the Roman garrison town named after Tiberias without having to climb the hillside and go cross country. By the time the sliver of the sun began to show over the eastern hills Micha could see in the distance the early-morning torches of a village on the lake ahead of him. Capernaum was awakening to greet the men as they returned with their nets and catches.

The increasing light revealed a large number of people heading from the lake toward the shore north of town. Micha continued to stumble over the small path near the road that swung around the town. He knew that his meager strength was nearly gone and that he would not be able to continue. It was, perhaps, best that he had to rest, since daylight would provide little refuge and cover for a man whose appearance would bring horror to a town. Finally Micha struggled to a vantage point above the town and watched as the crowd grew larger on the hillside. By midmorning it was evident that Capernaum and the whole region had gathered there.

Something inside him told him why the crowd had come. Edging along the fringe of an olive grove, Micha attempted to get closer. Between the terrain, his exhausted and deteriorating condition, and the desperate need to avoid discovery, his progress was painfully slow. It took the broken man several hours to circle the town and approach the edge of the crowd at a safe distance.

Periodically the leper had to pause, and when he did, he observed that one Man was the focus of attention. Micha could see Him gesturing toward the hills and sky. Little children, playing quietly, crowded around His feet. They brought back a bittersweet flood of memories, for he knew that surely Nattan would have been among the children if it had been Beth Zor. Through his tears the leper could barely see the face of the Teacher, but what he saw convinced him that it was a good face. Surely, if there was any good on earth at all, that Man would not turn him away.

Suddenly, in midafternoon, the crowd began slowly to disperse. A large group still surrounded the Teacher, though, and despair swept over Micha as he realized that Jesus might not return by the road to Capernaum. *What if He was to get on one of the fishing craft and cross over toward the Decapolis?* he thought desperately. *What shall I do then? Or what if He decides to walk around the lake along the north shore? How shall I ever catch up with Him?*

Micha grew desperate. He realized that his condition would not allow him to chase the Prophet all over Galilee. He would not survive another series of searches of the type he had already endured. Today was his only chance. If the power of Elijah moved again in Israel, he would have to find it immediately or die. In a last grasp of despair the tanner-leper of Beth Zor crashed down the hill from his hiding place toward the remaining crowd by the shore.

While he was still some way off one of Jesus' followers named Thaddaeus looked up to see the horrifying sight of a staggering corpse approaching the Master. The young man screamed, "Away! Away from us!"

Suddenly Thaddaeus felt a strong hand catch his wrist. He turned to see Jesus firmly holding him as the crowd began to fall back in terror. Without hesitation Jesus walked toward the leper. Someone cried out, "No, Master, no!" Jesus turned to him in a way that betrayed extreme emotion.

"Peter, put down that stone!" The disciples were surprised at His command, for He had never spoken to any of them that way before. Out of love, but not understanding, Peter let the stone drop to his feet.

When Jesus turned back to Micha He saw that the leper had already fallen to his knees, arms raised, to shield himself from the expected barrage of stones. "If You would desire, You could make me clean," the man said in desperation.

Suddenly Micha sensed somehow that he should be feeling something in his right hand. Struggling to see through his tears, he looked at the strong hand of the Carpenter holding his rotten stump and unwinding the filthy cloth wrapped around what remained of his hand. His natural reaction was to try to pull back as Jesus revealed his decay. Micha heard several of the women cry out in terror and noticed a man turn to retch at the sight. Again he attempted to pull away and cover his shame, but Jesus would not let him go.

Finally, Jesus dropped the filthy bandage and said as He held the rotten flesh, "I want nothing more, my friend. My Father's absolute will is this also. Be clean, as you desire."

For a moment silence reigned on the shore as the words of Jesus echoed through eternity. Then a woman gasped, and Micha looked down at his hand as Jesus released it. It was a hand fit to prepare parchments! The flesh was young and vigorous. Micha felt Jesus take his new hand and gently touch his face. He detected not a trace of a blemish anywhere. Suddenly the tanner realized that he couldn't even feel the bruises of the wound on his shoulder from the stone the day before, or his thirst.

Micha sensed that every fiber of his being was young and vibrant. Springing to his feet, he began to tear off the shameful and rotten robe in full view of the crowd. He turned to see Jesus laughing and smiling, and Micha also began to laugh and cry.

At last, as he stood naked before the Master, Jesus kicked away the old leprous rags and took a small outer garment off to hand it to Micha so that he might cover himself. Micha accepted the gift and rejoiced as he wrapped himself in it. Then Jesus stepped forward and placed His hands gently on the tanner's shoulders. "My friend, the Law is plain. I command you to show yourself to the priest without delay. Go at once to make the offering that Moses prescribed."

"I will, I will!" Micha replied with joy. "And may the Holy One be praised for what You have done this day!"

As Micha turned toward the hillside to retrace his way to Jerusalem he heard the voice of Jesus, calling again, almost in humor, "My friend, take the road!"

Of course, Micha almost blushed as he thought, *I am no longer an outcast.* "Yes, I will," he said over his shoulder, "and thank You again, good Master. Glory be to the sacred Name for You this day, Jesus of Nazareth!"

Part III

BACK FROM THE DEAD

∴

Micha rejoiced as he raced south toward Jerusalem. He had long forgotten the exhilaration of running. The breeze caressed his new flesh as he hurried along the western side of the lake. Whenever he felt winded, he stopped and slowly admired the strong new hands and fresh new skin, then, revived again, he would spring to his feet to run on down the path.

Once, as he rested, a sudden pain seized him. He wondered if the miracle was but a dream and he would awaken to find his dead flesh again. In terror, Micha decided he had to prove to himself that it was no dream. The tanner ripped off Jesus' cloak and jumped headlong into the lake. The cold water quickly convinced him that it was no dream, for every portion of his skin tingled as he scrambled up from the water again. Then, wrapping the robe about his nakedness, Micha continued on his happy journey, leaving his fears and doubts in the icy water.

When the sun began to sink over the hills of Ephraim, Micha found an olive grove to rest in. Through the canopy of leaves the stars of Israel twinkled once more. It seemed that God was again on His throne. The darkness pulsed out heaven's acceptance. An ancient psalm broke from Micha's lips. He remembered how often the Temple songs had enriched his days at the shop in Beth Zor, but no one sang in the caves of death.

Micha awoke to the warming sun and continued on his way to Jerusalem. It was midafternoon of the third day of his journey when he reached the brow of Mount Scopus and viewed once again the sacred Temple mount. The tanner drank in the beauty of the hill as he tried to convince himself that he could once more enter the holy site. Determined to reach the Temple before the gates closed, he hurried down the hill toward the Kidron Valley and the Golden Gate entrance on the east. One hope dominated Micha as he crossed through the court of the Gentiles. He wondered if it would be possible that Shemai, the priest who had condemned him, would be on duty. Micha recognized that it was only a remote possibility since the Levites served in rotation, but he dreamed that he might confront again the one who had pronounced him dead.

Finally, as Micha approached the gate between the Court of Men and the Court of Women, he asked an official if Shemai the priest might be serving in the Temple. Much to his surprise the man answered, "Why, yes, he does happen to be on duty this week. Do you want me to find him?"

"If you would bring him here to me, I would appreciate it," Micha responded. Micha knew that until he was pronounced clean and made sacrifice, he could not approach the Court of Men. He would not again be a "man" until proclaimed so by a priest.

In a few moments two priests approached the portal together. Shemai had just concluded assisting with a sacrifice and held his hands out to dry them after the ritual lavering. The first priest pointed to Micha, and Shemai looked curiously at the man dressed only in an outer Galilean robe standing among the noisy crowd in the Court of the Women. As the two met, the priest looked a bit confused, as though he was trying to place the stranger who stood before him.

Finally the priest said, "Yes, my son, I am Shemai. Should I know you?"

Micha slowly responded, "No, I don't assume you would remember me, for I was never to stand before you again. I am Micha, son of Joses, the tanner of Beth Zor. I presented myself to you when—"

Shemai gasped. "Micha? The tanner? This cannot be, for I myself condemned you according to the Law. You stand here today as a new man! How can this be?"

"The Holy One (blessed be He) has visited Israel again. I

have been made new! The prophet of Nazareth has taken my curse, and I live again!" Micha's voice began to rise as he recited the wonder of his healing, and the crowd around the two men began to notice that something out of the ordinary was taking place.

Shemai reached to take Micha's hand to lead him to the Chamber of the Lepers. It was one of four special rooms at the corners of the Court of Women. The other three served as storage for sacred oils, an inspection site for wood (so that all materials used in Temple service might be certified to be worm free), and a room reserved for those who had taken the Nazarite vows. The Chamber of Lepers was on the northeast corner and was for those who assumed that they had been cleansed from the living death.

Once inside, the priest slowly inspected Micha several times. It was as though he was desperate to find just one trace of the leprosy. Not that he desired more pain for the victim, it was just that no one had been cleansed from leprosy in Israel since the days of Elisha. Shemai could not believe that he was looking at the living proof of a new prophet.

Finally the priest spoke, but his thoughts seemed slightly disjointed. "Now, Micha, it seems that you truly have been cleansed and there is a procedure for such occasions. Uh, you are to, uh, go out and bring back a sacrifice. Yes, a sacrifice. No, you are to bring a bird. No, two birds. Yes, two birds, just field birds, ah, common birds. Go now, take this net here and bring the birds to me, and I will meet you at the gate of the men. Go now, quickly!"

Micha ran from the room as the priest stood momentarily stunned at what he was about to do. When Shemai finally left the room another priest approached and asked him anxiously, "Shemai, why did that man run from the Chamber of the Lepers with that net? Did you send him out?"

"Yes, I did, Joab. I sent him to catch two sparrows."

"You don't mean—"

"Yes, the man was a leper. I pronounced him so myself in

this very place. And now he has returned whole."

Joab pursued Shemai across the courtyard. "How could this be?"

"I don't know. Help me to remember the procedure of Moses for such an occasion. I never dreamed that in my day I would perform this ceremony, and now I find I barely recall what I am to do." Shemai looked perplexed as he struggled with the weight of the responsibilities of his office. "I, uh, must get some hyssop and a clay vessel."

"I will assist you if you desire," Joab responded. "I would be honored to be part of this ceremony." Shemai nodded as Joab continued, "The law, of course, requires water from a moving source, so I shall bring living water from the Gihon Spring . . ." Joab turned to get a pitcher for the water.

The court began to stir as the rumor spread that the priests were about to perform the ceremony for the cleansing of a leper. Someone stated that perhaps they should consult old Annas, the recently retired high priest, but others immediately asked why that would be necessary. Annas may have been a cagey and powerful figure, but he had no authority above religious law, and it was very specific about what to do now. The consensus was that Shemai should proceed without further delay.

Soon they had everything ready for the required sacrifice and the crowd waited with great expectancy for Micha to reappear. People slowly pushed against each other, maneuvering for a better vantage point. Some stood on the pedestal bases and clung to pillars in order to view the spectacle. Finally someone called out, "There, at the gate, that must be him!"

The faithful turned to see a young man carrying two sparrows in a reed cage into the courtyard. Many doubted out loud that he could be the one, for he was much too healthy to have ever suffered from leprosy. But then others whispered, "What do you expect? If he has been healed, then what did you expect?" Others chided, "Don't the Scriptures state that even Naaman the Syrian had skin as a child after his healing?"

But most refused to believe that Micha was the one about

to offer sacrifice. To their surprise, Shemai stepped forward and led him to the table where the implements of sacrifice waited. On the simple table stood the earthen bowl, a sprig of hyssop, a small scarlet cord, a cedar branch without greenery, and the pitcher of water that Joab had provided. The old priest took the reed cage and placed it upon the table. Then Shemai lifted his hands and intoned, "Micha, son of Joses, this day you have presented yourself to the Lord for the intention of redeeming the years of service to the Most High you have lost. You were sent forth from this place with the pronouncement of damnation because of the leprosy that had come upon you. For His purpose the Holy One (blessed be He) has chosen to deliver you again unto life and the living. Our father Moses received the sacred word, and this day we fulfill the command. . . ."

The priest stepped back and handed the earthen bowl to Joab. Shemai then poured the water from the pitcher into the clay vessel. Then the older priest reached into the reed cage and captured one fluttering sparrow and turned to hand it to Micha. "I now command you to slay this bird for the price of your uncleanness and pollution."

Micha felt the quivering terror in his hands. Glancing at the table for a sacrificial knife but seeing none, he then looked confused at the two priests who stood before him. How was he to kill the bird? The observing crowd strained in suspense.

"There is no implement for its death," Joab said firmly. "The law requires that the leper is to wring off the head of the bird with his hands. . . ."

Micha was horrified. His whole life as a tanner had been shaped by the teaching of his father Joses. His reverence for the creature was ingrained deeply, and the idea of mutilating the trembling sparrow went against every fiber of Micha's nature. But the law was explicit. Micha closed his eyes to contain his tears as he pressed his thumb against the neck of the sparrow and tore off the little bird's head. The sensitive, newly created hands of the gifted tanner felt the feathers and sinew and flesh and bone as the bloody mass dripped into the water. Eventually

Micha dropped the carcass into the bowl and stood with his hands dripping at his sides.

Shemai took the sprig of hyssop, the cedar branch, and the scarlet cord, and swirled them together in the water and blood. Then, with an ancient prayer, the priest splattered the mixture on Micha seven times. The crowd fell back as they avoided being splashed with it.

When the priest finished the seventh dipping he proclaimed, "And now, Micha, I return you to the living. You are to come again to Temple after seven days but not until you have shaved all of your body and washed yourself in living water. You then are to return with two lambs and a ewe along with flour and oil for the trespass redemption. You shall have the blood of one lamb placed upon your right ear, your right thumb, and your right great toe. If you are too poor for this, the Lord has provision for one lamb and doves for your payment and final restoration. Go now, son of Joses, return to Beth Zor your home until you return again according to the words of Moses."

Dripping with feathers and blood, the young man turned and the crowd parted before him as he walked out of the Temple precincts. Staring people strained to see the curious sight as he left the Court of Women through the gate into the Court of the Gentiles. Some of the God-fearers had stood upon pillar pedestals to observe the strange ceremony farther in the Temple, for they could not enter themselves.

Working his way through the crowd, Micha finally exited the Temple gate and began the journey to Beth Zor. Micha felt dirty and sticky and smelled of blood as it dried in the late sun, but he sang aloud psalms of praise. Children stared at the strange sight of a half-dressed man dripping with blood and singing to the brilliant blue sky.

As the sun neared the horizon the tanner of Beth Zor approached the village streets of his childhood. The little alleys were strangely deserted, for none had yet heard of the miracle for the son of Joses. Micha smelled the familiar meals in the street as he approached the home of his fathers.

Back From the Dead

Suddenly he came to the door of his former home. He heard the beloved voice of Esther singing the Bracha (blessing) of the meal inside. A child's voice mingled in the prayer. For a moment Micha, the tanner of Beth Zor, paused as he tilted his head toward the mezuzah and kissed the doorpost of his home.

DAUGHTERS OF ISRAEL

°°
°

Many Christians do not fully understand the Gospel stories because they lack a real knowledge of second Temple culture. New Testament Judaism provided the foundations for Christianity. We too easily wish to translate things into our own terms. (It's interesting to see how this fact demonstrates itself in artistic representations. Northern European painters often portrayed Bethlehem or Nazareth as being Amsterdam or Warsaw.) Translation is necessary to help the story come alive, but translation always diminishes the essence of a message.

Two areas of difficulty for contemporary Christians revolve around the role of women in Judaism and the absolute burden of the "matrilineage" chosenness.

First, to this day, many women do not understand the scriptural prohibitions regarding a woman's monthly cycle. They are tempted to call it "the curse" even without a misreading of Leviticus 15. Why would the Lord hold something against a woman that she had no control over? Misunderstandings like this easily cause resentment.

But if God is good there must be a solution. Most observant Jewish women know what it is—the dilemma is resolved by Rosh Hodesh. Once a month the Jewish calendar has a minor celebration related to the lunar cycle called Rosh Hodesh. It commemorates the new moon and reminds Jewish women everywhere that they carry the great privilege of being the repository of life. The logical conclusion is that God does not curse a woman for being a woman, rather He gives her a brief respite from common spiritual requirements. Rosh Hodesh is a cyclical reminder that God has so honored women.

Daughters of Israel

Another tension between modern Christianity and the Gospel realities deals with children and heritage. Many couples now choose not to have children. How is it that so many Bible characters literally pleaded with God for children? Why did they view barrenness as such a curse? I believe we can explain it this way.

Premise 1: God chose Israel. (And an unspoken corollary requires that in order to be chosen you must choose to be chosen).

Premise 2: God promised that Israel would continue as a people.

Conclusion 1: God needs Israel to continue, otherwise He apparently has lost control of His universe.

Conclusion 2: If a Jew does not have children, he or she has not done his or her part in continuing the race and is actually helping to end it—and that tears God off His throne.

Having Jewish children is to some, therefore, an issue of cosmic responsibility with universal implications.

Understanding opens up new insights into the following events at Capernaum.

DAUGHTERS OF ISRAEL

⁙

The ruler of the synagogue was a pious man named Jairus. The Capernaum synagogue was an important one. It was not a small minyan with the minimum quorum of 10 men. No, the community of the faith at Capernaum was the most prominent in the region. To serve as defender of the faith at Capernaum was a sacred duty and honored privilege. Jairus' decisions created repercussions all the way to Jerusalem herself, and he performed his role well.

Life was good for the ruler of the Capernaum synagogue. God had blessed him with his fine wife, Sara, and his daughter, Hannah. Hannah was completing childhood, and for more than two years Jairus and Sara had put her to bed with dreams of a soon-to-be-determined husband. Nearly a woman, her dowry would be offered in negotiation with the family of a worthy young man. Of course, as daughter of the ruler of the synagogue, her parents would have the pick of the crop of available young men in the region.

Lamps would flicker into the evening as they discussed possible husbands for their treasured daughter. "I have recently been considering Levi, son of Joseph the potter," the father said one night. "He is from a strong family and a good student of Torah for a young man."

"Oh no," Sara replied, "his family is good, but too poor, and our little girl will not be stricken with that burden. I will not hear of it. I have been discussing young Mattathai, the grain merchant from Bethsaida, with Mother. It appears that his family is quite prosperous. He is a fine-looking young man. In fact, in some ways he reminds me of a young man named Jairus that I knew once upon a time—"

"You flatter me, but I would remind you that Mattathai has a notorious temper, and I will not trust my little girl to a man of that reputation," Jairus responded firmly as he stirred the coals of the fire. "No, Mattathai will never do. But I am sure the Holy One (blessed be He) will reveal to us the man who would bear our grandsons." And for the evening the discussion ended.

At times other things overshadowed the father's joy of Hannah's approaching womanhood. An itinerant teacher from Nazareth named Jesus, son of Joseph the carpenter, had recently created a stir at the festival in Jerusalem. The priests declared that He was potentially dangerous because of His revolutionary views. With the Roman heel heavy upon Israel the last thing the faithful needed was an insurrectionist stirring Rome from her garrisons to remind Israel that she was a slave nation. If this Man would only stay around Jerusalem, then Jairus would not have to worry about the situation, but for some strange reason Jesus seemed to find a more receptive audience in the Galilee and had, at times, even made Capernaum His refuge and retreat.

Jairus had to walk a delicate balance in his life. On the one hand he was primarily responsible to God for his leadership. In another area he was constantly aware of his people, their needs and desires. And beyond that he had to keep in mind the wishes of the religious leaders in Jerusalem. The Pharisees did not directly control religious life in Galilee, but they kept track of what was happening there—especially the activities of the new healer and prophet. Jesus certainly had a way of complicating life.

If Jesus came to Capernaum there was no telling what might happen. It seemed every time that He retreated to the lake that more and more of the curious of Israel would flock to see what would happen next. Soon the leaders of the Pharisees would appear, and the atmosphere of the little lakeside village would become tense as Jesus would have to deal with the challenges leveled at Him. Jairus did not need any carpenter-turned-teacher to make his responsibilities even more complex.

The Judean Chronicles

Recently Jesus had been gone and the village was back to the normal routine topics of weather, fishing, olive harvest, and speculation regarding the pending marriage of Hannah. But then tragedy struck.

One morning Hannah awoke with a fever, and as the day wore on she became listless. By evening her parents had summoned the local physicians, and they stroked their beards in amazement. Not often did that disease hit with such virulence. It was indeed a complicated case. Some recommended a compound of bat-dung and goat saliva. Others swore that boiled Acce leaf would provide a brew that would break the fever. Still others shrugged their shoulders in disbelief. All the famed doctors of the region seemed baffled.

By the third day Jairus and Sara had had their fill of cures and potions and physicians. Hannah was suffering enough without the interference of the doctors. Three long nights passed, and the child seemed to be slipping away. Jairus went out under the Galilean sky and pleaded for intervention from heaven, but the fever persisted and his little girl continued to wither away. Jairus' God was silent.

As the sun broke on the morning of the fourth day Hannah was, if it were possible, even more listless and nonresponsive. Sara had long since run out of tears. Jairus was desperately negotiating with God when a messenger interrupted him. "Sir, I am so sorry to disturb you," the man said, "but He's back."

"He's back? Who's back?" Jairus demanded abruptly.

"The itinerant prophet Jesus. He's back, and a crowd is waiting for Him on the path by the lake."

"And why should I care anymore?" Jairus demanded. "I haven't seen Him harm anything, and He certainly doesn't seem to be a threat to our people."

"But sir," the servant reminded him, "don't you remember that the word from Jerusalem is that this Man should not be allowed to preach?"

"Curse Jerusalem!" Jairus shouted. But then he was stunned at the implications of his rash reply. He had committed his life

78

to defending the faith of his people, and he was horrified that he would ever wish evil upon Jerusalem. But his daughter was dying. Didn't the priests care? Didn't that carpenter care at all that this was no time for a theological confrontation? Little Hannah was dying.

But then Jairus remembered the stories that seemed to be growing around the Man. Some were claiming that He was performing deeds such as Israel had not seen since Elisha. Could it be? Was it possible that the Nazarene could touch blind eyes and restore full vision? Something in Jairus wanted to believe. He immediately left the house to go down the hill to the shoreline path.

As the synagogue ruler hurried through the streets a crowd began to follow him. Apparently they assumed that he was going to confront Jesus. Shopkeepers left their wares and fishermen their nets. Those not already by the lakeside to greet Jesus were soon streaming after Jairus as he headed toward the shore.

The crowd drew back as the two men approached each other. Silence spread through it as Jairus stepped up to Jesus. Suddenly the crowd gasped as those in front saw the ruler of the synagogue kneel at the feet of the One Jerusalem had labeled as a heretic. "Teacher, I beg of You, my little daughter lies even at this very moment at the point of death. I beg mercy of You. Do You care about her? Could God respond to my plea through You?"

"Noble Jairus, take Me to her," the controversial Teacher replied.

Together the men turned toward where the prominent townspeople lived. The crowd fell in step behind the desperate father and the controversial Rabbi. Excited whispers raced through the crowd as it snaked up the road toward the home of the ruler of the synagogue. They were sure it would be a day, an event, to be recounted for years to come. What would the Temple leadership say about this?

Suddenly as the crowd pushed and shoved to see and hear better, the Teacher stopped and asked, "Who touched Me?"

What a ludicrous question. The mob was pushing from

every angle, and He wanted to know who might have brushed against Him?

"Who has touched Me?" He repeated.

A woman turned in terror. She was standing near the center of the crowd, close to Jairus and Jesus, but she had been pushing to get away while everyone else had been trying to get closer. The crowd focused on her as it became obvious that Jesus was looking right at her.

"It's Miriam—yes, that's it—it's Miriam, the wife of Malchus," one of the older women said. And sure enough it was. But she looked different somehow. She seemed much younger, more vibrant.

"Are you sure?" asked one of the old men, who was straining for a better look at the scene. "Yes, there's no doubt about it; it's Miriam," replied a village elder.

Miriam was notorious because of the dark secret of her life. More than 12 years before she had been a happy, fulfilled daughter of Israel who knew her role and place in the scheme of things. She was the wife of Malchus and mother of four children. It was what life was meant to be for her. She had been born for that purpose.

Then one day she began her monthly cycle. It alleviated her from the common ritual obligations until the bleeding ceased. But after a week, and then two, the flow continued. Soon she began to see the various territorial physicians, who could offer her nothing for her condition. Eventually she made the journey to Jerusalem so that Malchus might offer special sacrifice to encourage God to hear her prayers and restore her. But the bleeding continued.

Leviticus stated that any chair she sat upon became ritually unclean. Similarly, any table she sat at, and utensil she used, anyone she touched, any garment she wore—her presence polluted them and therefore made them ceremonially unclean. By the fact of her pollution Miriam became an outcast and a pariah among her village and family. No one could deal with her in any normal manner because of her curse.

Daughters of Israel

Of course, the unspoken question that lingered in the minds of all who knew her was what did this woman do to receive such judgment? One must have committed a particularly heinous sin to have fallen under such lasting condemnation and rejection. But poor Miriam did not know what she had done.

For months and then years she had walked under the Galilean sky and appealed to heaven that if she could not be cured from her problem, then at least could God have the decency to reveal to her why she should be condemned in such a manner? But the heavens remained silent, and only the gentle splashing of the lake broke the stillness.

For 12 years Miriam knew that God hated her but not why.

Then, as the rumors about miracles began to circulate in the region, a glimmer of hope grew in the woman's heart. Could it be that God would deal with her as He had so long ago with Naaman? If the ancient prophet would not reject the Syrian, perhaps the new one might not spurn a simple daughter of Israel. It was her only hope. So it was that Miriam had waited for Jesus' return to her district in the Galilee.

Her plan had been simple. She could determine God's response without a request. If she could but touch the Prophet she could know if God would grant her favor. Besides, if nothing happened she might be able to justify the failure by saying that God didn't really reject her, He just was oblivious of her, and she could go to her grave without that certain knowledge that He had refused her. A direct confrontation could bring honest rejection, while a surreptitious contact would always leave her a window of hope even if she didn't receive a blessing from the touch.

And so on that fateful morning Miriam placed all of her hope on her plan. As soon as she brushed her fingertips against the hem of the Carpenter's robe she knew that the years of agony were over. Once again she could rise and walk in the light of heaven. Miriam knew that she could go home to Malchus and her children. Now she could hold her grandchildren. God had understood her desperation and had responded.

But she did not count on getting caught. In horror Miriam heard the question "Who has touched Me?" She had rendered Him ceremonially unclean, and if He knew that He had been touched in that manner, He must certainly know who had done it. Suddenly she felt guilty. Again she heard the voice above the crowd, "Who has touched Me?"

Miriam's joy turned to terror as she turned and saw He was looking right at her. Something forced a confession from her heart. "It was I, good Master. I touched You."

Though the confession felt good on her lips she awaited the scathing rebuke. But then she felt arms around her. They were strong arms, good arms. "Oh, My daughter, your Father has never hated you," His voice said. "For 12 long years He has loved you and longed to embrace you. Your faith has made you whole; go in peace to your family."

He had forced her to confess because she believed she had injured Him. Her touch had never offended Him in any way, but she had believed that it did. For that she needed to confess. It appears that the wandering Rabbi was showing Capernaum that day that God is in a hurry to forgive.

But Jairus cut the scene short by interjecting, "Rabbi, I am pleased that You could help this woman, but my little daughter is even now at the point of death. This woman was not going to die during the next five minutes. I am sorry for her suffering, but she has lived her life. She has born her young for Israel. Hannah is just on the verge of womanhood, and I would hate God if He would allow my daughter to die just to save an old woman—"

At that instant a messenger hurried down the path, and Jairus turned to see who it was. It was Jonathan, his wife's brother. His face was anguished as he struggled to bear his message. "Oh, Jairus, I am so sorry," he cried, but Jairus just pushed him aside and turned to rush up the path. The ruler of the Capernaum synagogue made only a few brave strides before he collapsed against an old stone wall. In agony he dug his fingers into the ancient stones. Jairus' God had died. Inside him the pain cut like a cold blade to the heart.

Daughters of Israel

Is that what a man gets for serving his God? He had been faithful to the Torah and had served the ways of the fathers well for years. Did it account for nothing in heaven that he was a defender of the faith? Who needed a God like that?

Then through the pain and the blackness Jairus felt a strong hand on his shoulder. "Jairus, my friend, take Me to her," the Teacher said.

Why not? Jairus thought. *Where else do I have to go?* And slowly he returned home. Jairus had never before known a day when the lake did not sparkle and the wind did not sing. But now Capernaum was silent, and he saw nothing through his tears. The universe had crumbled and God was no longer in His heaven.

As the sad group drew near Jairus' home they heard a great commotion. Tradition stated that proper mourning required at least two flutes and three wailing women. But for the synagogue ruler's daughter there would naturally be much more than two flutes and three wailing women. Village people who cried out of their pain to the ancient hills filled the courtyard.

Jesus asked one of the mourners why she was crying. "Why? Why? What do you mean asking such a foolish question? A precious young daughter of Israel is dead and has left no name or legacy, and you ask why we weep? Have you no respect for the dead?" came the sharp reply.

"But she is not dead; she is only asleep, and I will wake her this day," Jesus answered.

"Asleep? What do you mean, asleep?" one of the mourners shouted.

"Yes," they all echoed.

"Look, Teacher, we may not be sophisticated like those you deal with in Jerusalem, but we know death when we see it!" a man in the crowd shouted. The mourners picked up the theme, and soon the courtyard seemed headed for a serious confrontation.

Jairus was horrified. His little girl was dead and these people wanted to argue. He would have dispersed them all in anger but Jesus took his arm and said calmly, "Take Me to her. Just believe and take Me to her."

83

The Judean Chronicles

And so Jairus pushed the mourners aside and entered the darkened home. In a back room they found Sara staring blindly at the wall and singing to the child while she held the hand that was now growing cold after burning with fever. The synagogue ruler came gently behind his wife and embraced her neck, but she was absolutely oblivious and continued to sing to her child.

Jairus then turned and saw Jesus. The Man was smiling! How dare He smile. First He invaded the privacy of their home, and then He had the audacity to smile in his daughter's death room. What was wrong with Him? Who was He to add to their torment?

But He *was* smiling. The Teacher was thinking to Himself, *Satan, most of the time My Father allows you to have your way. My Father proclaimed long ago that He would give you time to reveal yourself, and you have done a good job doing exactly that. But not this time. This time I am going to overcome you in the name of My Father and to His glory.*

For that Jesus could smile with great confidence. He stepped beside the grieving father and gently lifted the hand from her mother's grasp. With a voice that cut through thousands of years of sin, death, and decay, He spoke with absolute conviction, "My little daughter, I call you to wake up."

Hannah was an obedient little girl, and obeying the voice of this Man was no burden. She immediately smiled, sat up, and looked astonished at the small crowd in her room. "Mother, I am so hungry. Could we eat soon?"

Then Sara began to cry. Her little girl was alive again and her faithful husband's God was reborn, but this time He looked very much like an itinerant Galilean rabbi.

In the home of Malchus a great feast of rejoicing was also prepared that night, for it seemed that God had again visited Israel. After 12 long years (the whole lifetime of some little girls) God was back in His heaven . . . and He also walked the Galilee.

SIMEON'S ROTTEN MAT

•••

In order to fully appreciate the curious question that Jesus asked the invalid at Bethesda, we must clarify two issues:

1. The reality of Bethesda itself, and

2. The reality of the powerlessness of the Levitical demands.

Bethesda was one of several entrances to the Temple proper. The most prominent was the great Eastern Gate, generally the pilgrim's entrance and a dominant exterior feature that served as a site for great ceremonial occasions. The Eastern Gate emptied out toward the Kidron Valley and lay under the shadow of the Mount of Olives. Because the observant would approach the Temple mount from the east the gate seemed to provide direct access to the divine. All other entrances to the Temple floor paled in significance.

One of the lesser entrances was to the north and was called "The Sheep Gate." That portal provided access to the market site of the sacrificial animals for those who were not able to bring proper sacrifice with them. Bethesda was the outer porch directly adjacent to the north side of that marketplace. A southerly breeze on a warm day could render Bethesda nearly unbearable. In Jerusalem of the second Temple period there appears to have been little construction downwind of "The Sheep Gate." The site attracted the powerless and hopeless who had no other position or place in Temple life. The impotent found a refuge in Bethesda.

Why was this so? To many it appeared that God had rejected the invalid (Lev. 21:19-23). (An interesting question arises over God's intention in this matter. Was this rejection or a merciful release from common obligations that offered a

85

sort of "compensation" for the inequities of life?)

Therefore Bethesda became the home of the powerless, the hopeless, and the impotent. Its five porches were as close to the Temple as those whose destiny was beyond their control could ever come to the Temple. But, interestingly enough, Bethesda also provided a unique vantage point for observing the very worst excesses and blasphemous activities of the Temple market. Even the most sensitive heart would have become callous after 38 years of watching the things that went on there.

SIMEON'S ROTTEN MAT

⁞

Simeon watched the people around him that spring morning again just as he had done a thousand times during his decades at Bethesda. Some faithful pilgrim had journeyed to Jerusalem for a great feast and the "righteous" keepers of the way to God had just cheated him again. This time it appeared to be a northern Galilean, perhaps someone who worked in the olive oil industry. Simeon often passed the long days musing on the background and families of those who came to the sheep gate to be fleeced themselves.

Matthan, Simeon speculated. *Yes, I believe his name could be Matthan . . . Poor, trusting Matthan. Here you came all the way from Galilee to find your God, only to have His representatives cheat you again. Will you never learn? Will all the Matthans always be taken in as you are today? Didn't I see you last fall at the festival of Sukkoth when you came to the tabernacle outside of Jerusalem? Didn't you leave bitter that time also? You bring your lamb all the way from Galilee, only to have it rejected (for reasons that they need not explain to you, but will sometimes do out of generosity for your obvious "ignorance"). What was it this time? Perhaps a lump in the abdomen or a spot on a foreleg. It doesn't matter, for you are only an olive press laborer, and you don't know sheep. You have no way of knowing that the lump the priest found was part of a sheep's necessary anatomy. If the priest calls the spot a permanent deformity you have no recourse, for you certainly will not go all the way back to Naphtali or Manasseh without offering a sacrifice, now will you?*

Poor Matthan, hasn't it struck you as curious that they will offer you four shekels for a useless sheep? Have you never noticed that after you leave they will take your unacceptable sacrifice and put it in the back of the pen to sell as fit to some other unwary pilgrim? Of course the price to him will be six shekels, just as the one that you are purchasing now.

Oh, Matthan, I see you are having a bit of a problem in your money exchange. It seems the priest will not accept your two extra shekels, for you cannot certify that your coins are not pure enough silver. This presents no permanent problem for them, though, as they will soon direct you over to the table of exchange. There someone will gladly accommodate you at the rate of two to one.

It is, after all, Matthan, the way of the world—the way of the Temple. Do you really think that you are now fit to enter the presence of the divine as you mutter about the behavior of the "men of God"?

Yes, Simeon had seen it a thousand times, but it had little effect on him personally. After 38 years of rejection by God and His human agents, one more corrupt transaction was just a drop in the pool of futility that some called Bethesda.

A lifetime before Simeon had been a prosperous caravan tradesman. His caravans brought goods from Egypt and Greece. But many dangers lurked on the road, and not the least of them was the wrath of a merchant who knew you had swindled him with pottery represented as being from Babylon and actually cheap imitations from a cohort in Samaria. Simeon's ethics were not always appropriate but until one certain fateful day nearly four decades before, they had been profitable.

That one pottery transaction proved to be one too many, for the Edomite chieftain showed no mercy as he sent men to exact revenge from Simeon's caravan. Six of Simeon's servants perished, but the Edomite decided that death was too good for the swindler from Jerusalem. A swift blow to his lower spine left Simeon a permanent member of the fellowship of the broken who resided at Bethesda.

It wasn't the myth of the troubled waters that kept the invalids at Bethesda. Or the pagan shrine of a pagan healing god that had crept onto the site. One did not have to dwell by the side of the pool long before it became clear that there was no angel, no miracle, no divine intervention to be found in the five porches. But it was an excellent place to work on the guilt and charity of those who went to the Temple to find their own restoration. How could people approach God to ask for mercy with the voice of an unaided paralytic ringing in their ears?

Considering its hopelessness, Bethesda was pleasant enough. The community of the powerless understood each other, and the weather in Jerusalem was generally pleasant. Occasionally the summer days would be rank and oppressive, and at times the winter would bring a damp chill and a touch of sloppy, wet snow, but those days were the exception. The prevailing westerly or northerly breezes made Jerusalem pristine. But when the breeze came from the south, the heavy odor of the animal pens flooded Bethesda, and its residents were tempted to curse the God of the Temple who breathed such dank odor upon them.

But on one fateful day it was spring. Were it not for the masses who flooded Jerusalem for the Passover, Simeon would have considered it a good day. Thirty-eight years on a rotten mat helped him to understand his life well.

Pilgrim festivals were a mixed blessing. On the one hand they brought a whole new crop of faithful whose charity he could invoke. On the other hand, the sheep gate became chaos as many came needing sacrificial animals to appease their sense of guilt before God.

On that fateful Passover Simeon's musings abruptly stopped when he felt a shadow fall upon him. He looked up to see a Galilean standing over him. Simeon spoke to the stranger abruptly, "I'm sorry, but if you're waiting for me to move my legs so that you may pass by, you may be waiting for a long time. I haven't moved these dead stumps since before you were born, so I certainly won't be doing it today for you."

His bitter outburst brought no response. Instead the Man just stood there staring at him. Simeon grew irritated. Who was this rude pilgrim? Didn't they have invalids in Galilee? Why did He not move on?

"Look here, stranger, I don't know where you come from, but perhaps you've never seen anyone crippled before. Well, take a good look and then, if you don't mind, you might move on because you are blocking my sun. I have enough feeling in these old stumps to know when I am getting cold, and you are in the way." Simeon's frustration grew as he spoke. It seemed that the Man was bringing out the very core of his heart as he continued in frustration, "Go ahead, take a good look, and then move on to meet your God. Perhaps He accepts your type— He surely doesn't seem interested in anyone like me."

The old invalid leaned up on one calloused elbow to gesture toward the Holy Place and then collapsed in anger back upon his mat. But again the Galilean made no attempt to move. Perhaps he was deaf. Simeon shaded his eyes to read the face and discern if the Man did not understand him. He looked into the eyes. They were good eyes—penetrating eyes.

Finally the Man spoke. "Would you be made whole?"

"Would you be made *whole*?"

Of course, and the pool of Bethesda should be full of wine! The governor's daughter should peel grapes to drop into the mouths of invalids!

"Would *you* be made whole?"

And God should not hate guilty caravan owners! There should be Someone on the other side of the gate who accepted broken sinners! Men should not have to endure 38 years of dreams that could not be!

"Would you be made whole?"

The question rang in Simeon's ears again and again. He soon realized that it was the most penetrating question he would ever be asked, and truly the most basic question of his life. The Galilean had reached into the very depth of his life with five simple words.

Suddenly he realized that he really didn't know how to answer it. Wholeness would take him from his mat. He had been there so long that he no longer knew who he was apart from that mat. The mat was not much, but how could the Stranger ask if he wanted to leave his whole world and complete existence of 38 years? Apart from his mat, the world was very big and frightening.

Simeon's Rotten Mat

"Would you be made whole?"

Simeon did not know. His mat had become his reality. He could not remember any other. Nor did he know what he would be if he left it. The cripple felt that he had been born bad, that his life was destined to rejection and abandonment, so there was really no way he could know what "wholeness" even was. The mat, the porches, the pool, and the scent of the animal pens were his world. The powerless and hopeless had been Simeon's society for nearly four decades. The Stranger was asking him to quit being who he was!

The idea of wholeness was so alien, so foreign that he found it completely frightening.

"Would you be made whole?"

If it weren't for the eyes and the gaze that revealed a fathomless goodness, Simeon would have rolled over and cried. But something triggered a flicker of hope that life apart from the rotten mat could be good. The Galilean asked Simeon to reach for the unknown, but it seemed that a Man like that would not offer it if it were not good.

"Yes, yes I would," Simeon exclaimed. "But there is no miracle here. Thirty-eight years have taught me that Bethesda is outside the reach of heaven. I *would* be made whole, but I'm abandoned by God here . . . You go ahead, meet with your God. Please, just don't taunt me with Him anymore, I beg of you."

When the racking sobs subsided, Simeon looked through his tears, expecting the Man to have disappeared into the Temple. But instead he heard Him command, "Rise then! Take your rotten mat and walk in the light of heaven!"

Authority rang in that voice. The young Pilgrim said it could be done. Perhaps life could yet be good. Maybe God would yet touch the powerless.

Simeon glanced one last time into the Man's eyes and decided he would try. As he slowly rolled over he felt a surge of youth and vitality spread through his legs. What had been dead for so long was alive! He jumped to his feet, expecting to be unsteady, but his balance was absolutely sure.

Another invalid demanded in shock, "Simeon, what are you doing?"

"I'm dancing! I'm dancing in the arms of heaven! Praise to the Holy One," he exclaimed as he laughed and swung his mat above his head, "praise the Holy One this great day!"

Now he knew there really was a God. That there was acceptance. The world could be more than a narrow space by the pool.

Winded and laughing, Simeon quit spinning around and stared toward the gate to the Temple. No longer did it look like an impregnable barrier, but instead he felt a sense of invitation. After 38 years he ran past the astonished crowd at the gate to dance on the Temple floor. A Sabbath of deliverance had set the captive of Bethesda free.

JOHANEN,
ALMOST A MAN

•••

Galilee always lived in the shadow of Judea, but that was just fine for the people who lived there. They were simple, good people who loved the lake and the land.

The Sadducees may have controlled Jerusalem and its Temple class, but they had little effect on the Galilee. Zealots roamed the hills, but most of the common people around the lake were much too busy eking out a living to be politically involved.

The Pharisees sometimes tried to stir things up in the Galilee. But for the most part, the people of the territory survived on hard work and old values. Simple piety and an occasional pilgrimage to the Temple at Jerusalem comprised the religious life of the Galilean.

Wealthy cosmopolitan cities such as Sepphoris brought Hellenism and the Roman Empire to Galilee. But little villages such as Magdala and Tabgha were loved by those who lived there. Near Tabgha was the Roman garrison village named in honor of Tiberius. The lake itself is only 13 miles long and 8 miles wide, but the Romans built a small fleet to control the activities of the various factions around the lake region. In A.D. 135 the Bar Kokhba rebellion concluded with a surprisingly sizable naval battle on the lake.

Many of the Gospel stories revolve around the lake region, for it was there that Jesus found the greatest acceptance. The children who inherited the rolling hills of Naphtali and Isaachar were the original mid-Americans—simple, hardworking, straightforward people of the lake. And if the Galilee was Nebraska, then Tabgha was Brennerville—you know, just outside of Shelton, about an hour and a half from Omaha.

JOHANEN,
ALMOST A MAN

❖

Oh, Father, Father, lift me up again," little Andrew squealed as he scrambled up to his grandfather. The burly fisherman laughed while his youngest heir swung back and forth from his right arm. Eventually the young lad released his grip and tumbled back into the old man's lap.

Johanen mused as his tousled little Andrew snuggled against his robe, *Such should be the joy of every man, that he should hold his heritage with his own right hand. . . .*

It had not always been so for the fisherman of Tabgha. As a young man Johanen's right hand was his shame. . . .

To a man of the lake hands were the tools and skilled implements of livelihood. Any Galilean worth his salt could tie the knots to repair the nets almost while he slept off the previous night's efforts out on the lake. Generations of fishers had passed the skills of harvesting the lake from father to son. Every boy of the Galilee learned early the main trade of the region.

For hundreds of years Galileans had carefully pushed away from the rocky shoreline as the sun's last reminders painted the hills of Manasseh with the burning crimson. The crystal water glowed with the fire of sunset as the boats from all around the lake began to dot the rippled surface. Soon the men of the lake slid their well-worn nets silently into the black mirror in the ancient ritual of anticipation.

The Galilee water was much too clear to allow fishing during the daylight hours. Only darkness provided the cover that let a net trap the schools of fish. For generations fathers had taken sons onto the lake to teach them the ways of the Galilee. Old ones would point up to the myriad of stars in the velvet sky to retell again the story of the ancient covenant and how they, the sons of Abraham, had truly become as the stars of heaven. Young boys would stare in wonder at the constellations and ask such questions as "Father, which of those stars represents our family? Which area of the sky represents Capernaum [or Bethsaida or Tabgha]?"

And father after father, from night to night and year to year, would point to a beautiful but minuscule constellation somewhere in the shimmering vault of heaven and laughingly reply, "If one of them represents Tabgha, it must be in that very tiny cluster over there."

Only those who lived there loved that village. Nestled on the farthest point of the western shore, its few narrow paths were always the first to be warmed by the rising sun each day. With those first rays the village would come to life as the women would go to the shore to inspect the catch, to mingle in community, and to greet the weary men.

The morning ritual of the lake harvest was simple. One of the older men would stand in his boat to stretch after a long night of maneuvering, waiting, and work. Finally someone would speak. "Grandfather, you must be telling us that that lake has shared enough for one night."

"Aye, Lemuel [or Simeon, or Jonas, or Nathaniel . . .], she has given what she will for now. Blessed be the Holy One for the gifts of the night. Let us push on in, for Mother is waiting."

Someone in the bow of the boat would begin to sort the catch by size while others would fold the nets under the critical inspection of an elder. "Be careful there, Zacharias [or Jude, or Lamech . . .], you must hold the nets in your hands as though they are our lives. Your children live because of those nets—"

"Aye, Father. But someday, in the presence of the Holy One I am going to ask how it was that the men of the Galilee were cursed by the eternal law that nets should have more holes every morning than they do in the evening when we begin our work." And the six or eight men would laugh again at the ancient joke and stroke their beards at the truth of the statement.

By the time the boats reached the rocky shore the women would be waiting, anticipating the perpetual ritual. "How was it, Jonas [or Shemuel, or Timaeus . . .]," a woman would call across the water as the boat approached, "how was the lake this night?"

"Oh, she was good, my wife; she is always good. But she cannot be always generous, for at times the fish are naughty. Many refuse our invitation to meal!"

And the small community would laugh again at the thought, and they would love each other and their lake and the morning sky.

Old Johanen had known thousands of mornings like this in his life. And as he swung his young grandson on his right arm he remembered well one particular morning so long ago. The morning of his shame . . .

"Come, Johanen, wake up, my young son, for soon Father will return with the catch, and we must help him with the nets." The voice of his mother, Prisca, stirred the young child from his slumber, but he quickly jumped up to run to the lake, for he longed to be the first to the shore.

Johanen loved his gentle father, Timaeus, and missed his presence as he went to sleep each night. On the sixth day, the day of preparation, the lad reveled in the joy of having his father remain home one evening. He cherished that night, for it allowed him to lie beside Timaeus as he drifted to sleep and the dreams of childhood.

But all other nights Timaeus joined his brothers and uncles and cousins in seeking the generosity of the lake, and Johanen (along with every other young lad of the village and all the dogs of the region) was always determined to be the first to greet the fleet as they returned from the night's work.

On that one special day life changed—changed forever.

Johanen burst from his mat to race to the shore as fast as his five-year-old legs would carry him. He quickly saw his family's boat with Uncle Natan, Grandfather Laban, and his father,

Johanen, Almost a Man

Timaeus, at the stern deftly guiding the boat to the space among the rocks where that same boat had rested for generations.

"Father, Father, how was the night?" the young boy shouted across the shimmering mirror of the sunrise. "How many fish did you catch?"

"Johanen, my boy, the night was good and the Holy One blessed us again," the reply came in the strong voice that Johanen loved. "Now be careful, my son, let me guide her in . . . now you stand back with your mother and aunt Miriam, do you hear?"

Other young boys from around the village were running along the shore, and dogs were yapping. Women scurried to prepare the site for community sorting and sharing. None were to know that tragedy was soon to strike the house of Timaeus. It was a morning as any other.

Soon the kin of Laban had gathered and were ready to assist as Timaeus, Natan, and the others cast the nets to the shore and threw the evening's catch onto the mat prepared for the sorting. When they had emptied the craft the men would lift the old boat from the water. This would allow them to inspect the hull and to protect it from banging against the boulders as the afternoon winds came up throughout the region of the lake.

A good inspection of the hull and careful repair of the nets done every day would guarantee that the tools of the Galilee would serve a clan for many years. No self-respecting man of the lake would think of leaving his nets uncared for or his boat unprotected.

On that one fateful day they had absolutely no warning that any danger was imminent. The fish were scattered on the mat as usual, the nets were stretched to dry, and the teams of men gathered together, moving from boat to boat, lifting them from the water to shore.

"Let us now beach your vessel, Timaeus," Jehuda, one of the strong old leaders of the community, called to him. "Yes, your craft and then only two more and we put the night away."

Fourteen or 16 men gathered around the vessel of the house of Laban and gently rocked her on edge so that they could flip her over. This allowed the water to run out of the hull, lightened the load, and also gave the men a more secure hold upon the rails of the boat. With a rythymical "heave" that had been performed 10,000 times by the side of the lake, the men hoisted the vessel and began to walk her up onto dry land. But none suspected what was soon to happen.

Little Johanen decided that morning he was going to help his father. He ran to the point of the boat that was already on shore to grab hold of it and do his portion of the lifting. But just as he reached the point of the bow, he tripped on the wet rock and stumbled. As he fell his body collapsed right in front of his uncle Natan.

Natan struggled to keep his balance, and when he eventually stumbled, he started a chain reaction of tripping and falling by the men on the left side of the boat. One by one they struggled but could not keep the weight of the old vessel up, and it came crashing down in spite of the best efforts of the men on the other side of the craft.

Suddenly, from under the hull, came a horrifying scream. The men scrambled to their feet to lift the vessel, and as they at last moved it, they saw the terrified form of little Johanen writhing in pain, his right arm crushed.

In terror Miriam rushed to her child and began to scream. Timaeus ran around the boat and scooped up the small bundle and ran toward the village, but he had no destination. Had this been the days of Elisha, he would have run to the prophet, but his people had had no miracle worker for many years. Their little boy was broken, and there was no one to fix him.

The first days and nights were horrendous, but the little body began to compensate for the damage, and eventually the pain vanished. No feeling remained at all in the crushed and withered arm. Nature, in a way, was kind.

But what does a man of the lake do with only one good arm? How do you repair nets with only one useful hand? How does one be a man when he is broken?

As the years progressed Johanen grew and did what he

could, but he knew that he would never truly be a man with half of him dead at his side. He would steer the boat and sort the catch, but he was not capable of doing much of the work of the lake. Repairing the nets and lifting the catch from the water and hoisting the boats in the morning was beyond him. He did the best he could, but he knew he was not a man.

Temple ritual was also denied him. The law was clear regarding the restrictions for the crippled.

Many in Johanen's plight would have easily become embittered, but it just was not in him. He often was tempted to retreat into the pain of Job's wife, who demanded her husband to "curse God and die," but that just was not part of his fabric. He did not understand why this curse had fallen on him, nor why the law would not allow him to approach God as those who were whole, but he just could not bring himself to become hate-filled. Johanen would only find that the numbness in his arm usually caused him to retreat into his emotional pain.

As Johanen grew the deadness in his arm would at times affect his soul, but the gentleness of his heart always fought it. He could not help himself; he just would not let bitterness overwhelm him.

Childhood faded and Johanen existed as half a man in the region of the lake. The tenderness of his heart was legend along the shoreline, but though no one could explain why a tragedy like that should happen to a child as gentle as Johanen, there was also nothing that anyone could do to help him become a whole person.

That is—not until that wondrous Sabbath in Capernaum.

Many from around the lake had gathered in Capernaum because Jesus, the wandering rabbi of Nazareth, had come back to the town and was, by that time, famous throughout Israel. His recent return to the Galilee from the Jerusalem Passover had become known throughout the lake region. Rumors ran wild concerning the events that had transpired while Jesus had been in Judea. Some said there had been confrontations with the Sanhedrin after the rabbi performed mighty deeds in the

Jerusalem streets and taught radical doctrines in the Temple precincts. Others said that He had left the city under the threat of judgment and even possible execution for heresy.

All the men of the lake region gathered that morning in the synagogue of Capernaum to listen to the controversial prophet, teacher, and supposed healer.

Johanen was also there, sitting, as was his custom, off to the side of the rest of the men. Since the day of his becoming a man of the law he had never felt as though he was part of those who were "whole." He knew he did not belong out on the fringe of the room with the women, but he never felt that his place was within the inner circle of the building either. From a distance he had observed the rituals that honored the God who had visited a confusing judgment on a young boy so many years before.

The room stirred with the voices of those who led in the ritual and prayer. One could also catch the whispers and comments of those who wondered if the Rabbi would speak or reveal His intentions in any manner.

Suddenly one of the community leaders stood and demanded of Jesus, "Teacher, son of Joseph (if that is your father), we have heard that you desecrated the Sabbath while you were in Jerusalem. Tell us now, do you deny this charge?"

The room fell silent. All eyes turned toward the controversial teacher as He stood and spoke with a calm assurance, "My brethren of the Galilee, I know what you are thinking. You ask yourselves, 'Will He perform mighty deeds here, as we have heard of Him doing throughout Judea and the Galilee? Will He show His position on the sacredness of this day?'

"I see here a man of the Galilee, a man without fault but bearing the curse of a world that is not fair. You here, friend of the lake, I ask you to stand . . ." And with that Jesus pointed to the fringe of the room and Johanen.

Without thinking, without fear, Johanen stood with his arm tucked under his cloak, as he had done since childhood. He heard Jesus speak again. "Men of Galilee, I ask of you only one thing. Of what purpose is this day? Is it not given to us by the Holy One to be a blessing and not a burden?" The room stirred at His question.

The Rabbi continued, "You wonder how I feel the Father thinks of this day, and I now show you . . . My friend of Galilee, stretch forth your hand. . . ."

For a moment Johanen wavered. That arm had been his curse for many long years. It had been his burden. The dead stump blocked his way from being a whole man, from approaching his God without reservation. His greatest pain, he had kept it hidden since the day so long ago when the boat had crushed it.

And now this Stranger was asking him to drop all of his defenses and expose his great shame to all who watched. But something in the Man's voice stirred the flicker of hope that his soul had never surrendered. Something in His expression touched his tender heart and made him long to comply.

For a moment Johanen wavered, and then he flipped back his cloak with his left hand to reveal the mangled limb. Slowly he pointed his shattered hand toward the Nazarene teacher.

And from the moment that he first began to extend his hand Johanen sensed life and vibrancy in his dead arm. He could feel the strength of manhood pulse through the muscle and sinew and flesh and bone. Glancing down at his hand, he stared in amazement, then suddenly shouted, "Glory! Glory to the Holy One! I'm a man! I'm a man!"

All looked in amazement. The lake men had witnessed the power of God on that Sabbath in their synagogue. Some sang old psalms of praise while others snarled in anger at how Jesus had desecrated the holy day. Jesus' followers congratulated each other on the privilege of being His men, His honor guard. Women whispered frantically, and children scurried between legs to catch a better look at the man whose hand they had never seen. The whole region soon exploded with the news of the miracle performed for the son of Timaeus.

But, in that room,
in that place,
by that lake,
on that Sabbath

The Judean Chronicles

Jesus smiled broadly as Johanen held up the hand that had been so long his shame and shouted praises to the One who nightly watched over the boats of the Galilee and her men.

THE FAILURE

••
•

We miss the power of many Scripture stories because we are not familiar with the Eastern mind and traditions. The effort of learning a bit more of what a Jew is, what the texture of "Eretz" (the land) of Israel is like, and the interplay of the Hebrew language will receive rich rewards. The Gospel narratives will sing new harmonies that we did not previously hear.

One of the most beautiful and hopeful of all the Gospel stories appears in but a few verses in each of the Crucifixion accounts. The thief on the cross stands until the end of time as a message of great hope for all struggling sinners. But before we approach the sacred ground called Calvary, let us consider two realities.

First, we miss the power of many Bible stories because we do not understand the concept of names in ancient times. Names had power—even magic. They reflected the nature and destiny of their bearers. Kings would live in great fear that the day might inevitably come when a successor or conqueror might erase their names from the monuments of their accomplishments. Israel yearned for a "name" that would remain forever.

The Egyptian Book of the Dead focused on the names of the pantheon of gods the soul would encounter during its journey after death as it attempted to gain entrance into the Western Fields, the Egyptian realm of the dead. (If you knew a god by name you had immediate leverage upon him or her and could control the deity to your advantage more easily.)

Even in dealing with the Holy One the Bible writers constantly wanted to "bless the name of the Lord." Why the name? Why not just bless the Lord and get it over with?

The Judean Chronicles

What is the Eastern mind saying about the power of the name in all of this?

The answer opens up volumes of insights into Bible stories, but in itself it is a relatively easy concept. For example, your power and influence and relationship are entirely different if you look at someone and say, "Distinguished Professor of Near East Studies and renowned expert on Jewish Temple cult sacrifice . . ." versus "Hi, Jacob!" Titles and positions only tell us *what* you are, but your name tells us *who* you are. When I call you by name I have access to your heart that I am not otherwise granted.

And the reverse of that is just as important. If my name gets erased from memory, the horrifying question must be asked, "Did I ever exist?" Little wonder the Bible is filled with references teaching that God intends His people to never be forgotten. "Blessed is he whose name is not blotted out . . ." Four of the seven churches of Revelation 2 and 3 have their overcomers being promised something that revolves around a name.

Many Jews to this day, when speaking of an enemy of Israel, say the name with an oath: "Then Haman [or Hitler, or Goering, or whoever . . .], *may his name be stricken from memory, . . .*" And they will say of someone beloved: "Then my grandfather [or Abraham, or Moshe Dayan, or whoever] *of blessed memory . . .*" They also pray the Kol Nidre for the remembrance of the dead. Even the prayer of the Pesach Seder (Passover dinner service) is "zacher l'chaim"—*"remember us to life!"*

I desperately want you to know me, and I don't want to be forgotten.

The second insight we need to understand some of the issues surrounding the narrative of the thief requires one little lesson in Hebrew. Whenever the two-letter construct "lo-" (the letters lamed and aleph) appears in front of a word it reverses the meaning. My sons are *"lo-girls"* and black is *"lo-white."* The prophet Hosea reversed the names of the children who were not his (*Lo-ammi* and *Lo-ruhammah*) when he accepted or adopted them as his own (Ammi and Ruhammah).

Dag Hammarskjöld (who apparently never knew he was so

104

The Failure

Jewish) once wrote, "There are two types of men in the grave—men of promise and men of accomplishment."

The word *asah* means to fulfill or accomplish. The thief Lo-asah should have been "somebody," and he eventually made it.

Part 1

THE FAILURE

Lo-asah sat in the rancid darkness, idly twisting the end of the leather straps that encircled his ankles. Without thinking, he found himself again creating the binding of the tefillin upon his left arm. It had been years since his uncle had taught him the ancient and mystical patterns of what was called "the akedah" (the binding) for the tefillin tails of the phylactery. As a child Lo-asah's mother, Miriam, reminded him constantly that he was destined to be, like his father and his uncle before him, a Pharisee. She dreamed that his faithfulness to the details of religious law would be part of the efforts that might guarantee that Israel would never again be taken captive for disobedience. In generations past prophet after prophet had warned the people that if they disobeyed they would pay the price outlined in the curses of the covenant. When Babylon rolled in, serving as the judgment hand of God, some finally learned the lesson. After 70 years of captivity many Jews determined never to be caught disobedient again. Eventually their spiritual descendants would be called Pharisees.

When his father died in the great fire of Sepphoris the task of nurturing Lo-asah in the ways of the Torah fell to his uncle, Zadok. Zadok was an uncompromising man who taught the lad the meticulous details of law without apology and without passion. During the years of his childhood Lo-asah showed proper respect, but as he began to grow, his interest in spiritual things faded. The cold teachings of Zadok never filled the void within Lo-asah for the father he never knew, but the uncle continued to press the boy for more perfect fulfillment of the requirements of the rabbis.

The Failure

"Our people were taken into captivity at the hand of the uncircumcised for disobedience," the older man would say. "It is up to us, the defenders of the faith, to guarantee to heaven that Israel will never be faithless again." And so the lessons would continue. Young Lo-asah learned them well but always resented the fact that he was responsible when so many others seemed not to be. Why must he be burdened with such efforts when so many boys lived carefree lives? Why did the old God of Israel require of him such obedience when so many others lived lives of fun? It often seemed that the burden of righteousness was terribly inequitable.

By the time that Lo-asah became an adult under Jewish law and able to participate in synagogue and Temple life, the boy felt a terrible ambivalence toward it and his God. Much of him wanted to be good and fulfill his mother's dream, but a large portion of him enjoyed the company of the young boys of Sepphoris whom his mother had attempted to forbid as his companions. Often he would find himself coming home later than he should have because of the influence of Shemuel and Joses and the others. Though Lo-asah was never completely comfortable with all they did and with their Hellenistic entertainments, he found the village boys to be so much more enjoyable than the synagogue faithful. They usually accepted him for what he was and only occasionally urged him to participate in things that troubled his conscience. That was more than he could say for the faithful who never seemed to accept him. He knew he could never be good enough for those righteous ones and their demanding God.

It hurt terribly to read the disappointment in his mother's eyes as he grew away from being a simple, obedient child. He hated his uncle's lectures and the nagging of the synagogue leadership. Although he never intended to hurt anyone, he slowly felt himself drifting away from the imposed values of his childhood. One night in particular he realized how much he hated himself and how he did not understand any of his life. He had returned home from an evening with his city friends.

Zadok was waiting for him, and he saw his mother crying softly in the corner. It seemed that some of the town leadership had finally, after two weeks, pieced together the names of the boys who had tipped over the merchant Nathan's cart and injured his donkey. Zadok's stinging lecture rolled off of Lo-asah, as so many others had before, but he couldn't escape the haunting question of his mother, "Lo-asah, how could you do this to me?"

He hadn't intended to do anything to his mother. It had all seemed like a harmless prank, and he was truly sorry that it escalated into something damaging. Joses had laughed and Shemuel had taunted the injured beast, but the whole sight had sickened Lo-asah's sensitive heart. The young man broke down in tears of hopelessness when his mother finally said, "I do not know what to do with you. . . ."

That night as the bitter tears fell, two competing storms raged in Lo-asah's soul. A large part of him wanted to do well and never wanted to harm anyone, but he knew that he wasn't good enough no matter what he would do, and so it all seemed so futile. He knew his efforts would be of no avail, for nothing he tried would ever appease Zadok or Zadok's God. Half of him wanted to promise that he would never fail again and the other half reminded himself that his promises were useless. The hurting man/child ached over his terrible dilemma. He felt he should surrender to the inevitable failure of his life and just quit trying, but the gaze of the holy God was constant.

Sometime after that night Lo-asah understood that he was destined to rejection and that the best he could hope for would be that someday in eternity God would know that for a while he did try and maybe that holy God would not completely hate him.

And now, in a Roman dungeon, he lashed himself, for he obviously had not tried hard enough. In the darkness Lo-asah found that Zadok's demands were as ingrained into his soul as Zadok's patterns for the tefillin bindings were to his hands. Quietly Lo-asah sobbed.

None of it was supposed to end up this way. The mischief of boyhood with Shemuel and Joses had progressed into more

The Failure

dangerous activities. He never felt completely right about what he got into, but he also never seemed to have the strength to stand against his friends' disapproval either. Many times as they would be in the middle of some silly act Lo-asah wanted to leave and never have anything to do with their kind again, but they were his friends, and except for their complete lack of spiritual bent, they seemed to understand him. As long as he tried to please them they fully accepted him. If men like Shemuel and Joses were not to be his world, then who was? It was a sure bet that the privileged and righteous would never completely accept him. No matter how hard he tried, he knew that his efforts would come up short in the eyes of the holy ones. But still, it wasn't supposed to end up this way.

Damaging merchants' carts and stealing hides were the pranks of children, and as the young men grew they left behind such childish things. For quite a while the young band attempted to convince themselves that their actions were justified. If they stole from a merchant they were but correcting the inequities of an unjust world. "It isn't right that this man has so much and we have so little," they would say as they became drunk. The wine would give them bravado, and they would be off to share the wealth. Eventually they didn't need wine to trigger their greed. At times they would taste the surge of power that stealing gave them before they would even begin to drink. In their minds their crimes made them above law and granted them a freedom that they'd never known.

One day the childhood friends fell under the influence of Simon, a determined and strange criminal. Lo-asah had never met anyone so powerful. He was a strangely quiet man who spoke only when it served his purpose in dominating someone. The man's silence usually served him for words. Simon's presence evoked both fear and admiration. He had accomplished more than Lo-asah had ever dreamed. But Simon had something more than just the heart of the common thief—he seemed a man driven. His compulsion to crime frightened and yet intrigued Lo-asah. Though everything he did went against the grain of his own conscience, Lo-asah found a sort of admiration for a man who seemed so totally free of conscience. Simon did his deeds with no regard for others. At first it repulsed Lo-asah's sensitivities, but at the same time it also held a strange appeal to him.

It seemed that all of his life he had struggled against two competing forces in his heart. Lo-asah never wanted to hurt others, but at the same time he never seemed capable of anything else. He longed for freedom from his internal struggle. It was as though Simon offered that release. Lo-asah only wished that the man was not so violent in his methods.

Then one night it all seemed to be justified. Some of the band were bantering back and forth about what to do next. A few of them were getting drunk around the small fire when Simon finally stood and spoke. The rabble fell silent as the fire reflected in the Zealot's intense face. "I say it is enough! You are all small men and have no dreams. You care only for the wealth of your fellow Jew, and you justify the harm you do to his daughters by your drunkenness. Not I! No longer. I am a man and a son of the Maccabees! I will raid no more with cowards. I am weary of petty crime as my life wastes away under the heel of Rome."

With that Simon spat on the floor as if to clean his mouth of the vile taste of the hated word. Even the most inebriated of the band fell silent at his outburst. It was evident that none would challenge him. Lo-asah almost trembled with fear and excitement. He was afraid of Simon but also yearned to share such passion and fire. Simon's words stirred a response in Lo-asah's heart as he listened. "I will no longer offend my brother of Israel," Simon stated. "I am shamed that I have fallen to such childish efforts. What has it gotten any of us? If we had sons, what would we tell them? That we have lived only to raid the storehouses of the wealthy and squander the spoil in drunkenness? Not I! No longer! I am called to greater destiny. If I am to be punished for any crime, let it be one that gives me a name of honor. I vow this night that I am going to scar the oppressor. His wealth shall be mine and his pain my rejoicing."

The Failure

Simon's eyes slowly scanned the silent group. Every man weighed the consequences of the moment. No one challenged him. No one spoke a word. No one dared breathe as Simon's hand went to the knife that had just been used to carve the stolen goat. Holding the blade aloft in the silhouette of the fire, the Zealot proclaimed, "Rome shall pay for making the people of Simon of Sepphoris slaves in their own land!"

The drunken group responded in raucous support, and Lo-asah, in fear, also joined in the chorus. He was horrified at the prospects of confronting the Roman occupiers, but he had always taken the path of least resistance, and that fateful night around the fire it did not seem to be the time to begin to stand for up for himself.

Thus truly began Lo-asah's journey to the Roman garrison dungeon in Jerusalem. All those scenes flashed in his heart as he idly twisted the leather Roman straps around his left arm. In the darkness the ingrained ancient prayer almost escaped his lips as he twisted the bindings: *"Baruch atah Adonai, elohenu melech ha-alom. . . ."*

But Lo-asah found that the prayer died in his mind, for at that very moment Shemuel burst forth with a string of profanity. He was cursing Rome and the cowards of Israel and Simon and anyone else he could lay his tongue to. Out of habit, as he had done all his life, Lo-asah joined in the cursing, but only for a moment. Instantly it all seemed so futile. He lapsed into silence, for in the darkness he clearly saw his life.

The young boy of promise in the synagogue of Sepphoris had never had an original idea in his life. He couldn't think of a time when he wasn't following someone else. As a child he had obeyed Zadok and as an adult reflected Simon's irrational greed. Lo-asah abhorred himself.

It wasn't supposed to come to this.

Soon the guards would drag Shemuel and him out to face some lower-level Roman official to receive a mock trial. Lo-asah assumed he would be sentenced to the quarries for his crime. After all, no one was hurt and they had done only minor damage to the Roman barracks before the returning garrison caught them. It was all so petty, but it was also so very stupid. He even reasoned that a few years in the quarries might teach him a lesson that would become the foundation of a life worth living. Whatever was on the other side of his sentence couldn't be any more futile than the purposeless life he had already known.

Lo-asah sat in silence as Shemuel's profane oaths died down. He decided that if he was going to curse anything he would curse his own stupidity. *Someday,* the young man thought to himself, *I will stand a man. Someday I will show myself to be worth something in this world* . . .

In the dank Roman hole of Jerusalem Lo-asah knew that it was not supposed to end this way.

Part II

THE FAILURE

Lo-asah believed it must be early morning when he stirred from his troubled sleep. His back ached from the cold stone floor under the rotten straw, but it was decidedly better than when they had been thrown into the cell almost two weeks previously. For days he had faded in and out of consciousness because of the beating he'd received after their arrest in Tiberias. Still, that probably had been a blessing. The Roman soldiers had taken them to such a hellish place that he was glad he had not been fully aware of it. The unconsciousness from the beating had allowed him to become gradually accustomed to the stench and oppressive darkness.

In Tiberias the guards had only slapped the prisoners and lashed them together for the two-day journey to Jerusalem. By the time they arrived at the Antonio Fortress some of the Romans had grown increasingly impatient with their duty. The last thing they wanted to do was drag a couple of low-life Jewish thieves to the provincial capital. They wanted "real duty, fit for real soldiers and not this nursemaid assignment of escorting petty criminals for some fat judge in Jerusalem." After two days of dust and sun and rocky paths the mood of the soldiers had grown ugly. They wanted some real action.

Their attitude was understandable. Attacks by Zealot bands and terrorists had been on the increase, and the Romans were feeling more and more that the kettle of Judea was about ready to boil over at any moment. The Roman Senate was growing impatient, and though the Jewish leadership acted as though they wished to mollify their conquerors, there wasn't a Roman soldier this side of Damascus who felt safe alone at night. Rumors of Jewish deliverance spread everywhere. According to many in Israel, the Messiah would soon march in triumph to Jerusalem. Yes, David had been dead for a thousand years, but the talk of his spiritual son seemed almost too powerful to ignore. The soldiers knew that dreams can be more dangerous than reality.

The Roman soldiers took out their fear and uncertainty on Lo-asah and Shemuel in Jerusalem. The captain of the garrison decided that the beating of a couple of petty criminals would be a good way to vent the intense pressure on his men, and so he overlooked their abuse of the new prisoners from the Tiberias sector.

Lo-asah passed the first few days of his Jerusalem captivity drifting in and out of consciousness. Barely aware of the odor of the room where men had lived and rotted and died, he did learn that the rats were more active at night, allowing him to sense, despite the ever-present darkness, the passage of the days. By the time he could have really smelled the rancid filth of the hundred prisoners who had lain in that spot before him he was accustomed to the stench. His beating, therefore, saved the effort of retching up the small amounts of stale bread and broth that Rome, in all her generosity, provided him.

Lo-asah tried to roll to another position to relieve the pressure on his left side. In the darkness he heard the dripping of water in the damp cell and the unintelligible and muttered curses of Shemuel, who fitfully slept just a short distance away. Seventeen men of all ages crowded in that hole. Most were hardened criminals who would have ended up in a dungeon with or without Rome. A few were stuck there at the whim of a petty official, and they spent their days in prayers for deliverance. (Of course, their petitions met derision and scorn from the prisoners who had long ago abandoned any belief in Israel's God. When they cursed the faithful, Lo-asah echoed their scorn, for he didn't know what else to do.)

After recovering from the beating enough to be conscious, Shemuel and Lo-asah passed time by either cursing their leader, Simon, or yearning for him.

The Failure

"I know he will come for us," Shemuel would say. "He truly is a son of the Maccabees, and Rome will run in fear from him someday."

"We are his men," Lo-asah would reply, "and he will not abandon those who fought in his cause. He will find a way to get us out of this cursed place. . . ."

That was the dream, but usually even in the darkness the two men knew the reality. Simon had deliberately left them to be caught by the returning guard so that he might escape himself. When they allowed themselves to recognize that fact, they both cursed the miserable hide of "Simon the coward."

Simon had hatched a plan to embarrass the Roman garrison at the Galilee outpost of Tiberias. It was only a day's journey from Sepphoris, and he had plotted their attack for a night that the Roman forces would be out scouring the hills for Zealots. "It will be a great blow to our mighty guests," he stated sarcastically. "The fox will be out looking for his prey, and the lamb will be destroying the fox's den!" All the band had joined in laughter at the thought of Romans returning to their lakeside barracks, only to see their storehouses and possessions going up in smoke. The faithful of Israel from all around the lake region would be able to see, far into the night, the smoldering affront to the eagle of Rome. The mirrored flames might even ripple to all ends of Israel.

More wine and laughter gave the inexperienced band of terrorists courage, and good planning succumbed to bravado. It really hadn't been a bad plan, it was just that the information that they'd coerced from one of the prostitutes of Magdala was not completely accurate. The young Roman soldier's bragging, it ended up, was somewhat overblown. On the fateful night that Simon's men slipped into the garrison they were surprised in the middle of ransacking the barracks by the return of the larger portion of the Tiberias Roman contingent. The soldiers had not gone toward the Jericho hills but had sent only a small number out on patrol while the rest had remained close to the port.

In the unexpected commotion Simon showed very quickly

that it would be every man for himself. Lo-asah and Shemuel had the misfortune of being the ones who had volunteered to burn the stables. It would have been a glorious feat, but the wall on that end of the compound was much too high to escape over, and the returning soldiers had trapped the men.

And so it was that two young men came to lay in the rotting straw of the dungeon in the Jerusalem stronghold of Antonia.

In the heavy darkness Lo-asah knew that Simon would not deliver him. Again he felt a failure. Some great Zealot he had turned out to be. He had never even gotten away with stealing a Roman spear or bridle, let alone put a knife in the heart of Israel's enemy.

The young man thought of his mother. He was quite sure that she would no longer speak his name aloud. After all, he had shamed her. If he was to be punished for some patriotic deed or some crime in the name of Israel it would have been one thing, but to be condemned for having a Roman bridle in your hand while your friend is trying, without success, to get the grain to burn in the stables is not much recommendation for bravery. If he had been sober he might have figured out a way of escape. (But then, if he had been sober he might have seen through Simon's facade and realized that it was all a sham in the name of patriotism. Simon was also only a common criminal and a coward who tried to justify his life under the guise of patriotism.) Lo-asah cursed himself and his weakness.

Zadok, his father's brother, would surely guarantee that his name would be removed from the rolls of the synagogue faithful. They would not tarnish the holy reputation of those who worshiped there with the name of a common thief. No one in Sepphoris would ever speak his name again. (And no one outside of Sepphoris knew him.) It would be as though he had never been born.

Lo-asah was tired of being brave. He was tired of dreaming that Simon was strong and that he would deliver them. He was tired of Zadok's disdain and the silent tears of his mother. He was tired of the curses of the men around him and the prayers

The Failure

of those whose God did not listen and did not care. And most of all, he was tired of his life.

Part of him still wanted to dream that he would get out from under the curse of Rome and make something of his miserable existence. But the dank, rotten, musty straw was his only reality. The God of Israel seemed distant and uncaring. Very much against his wishes the little criminal of Sepphoris began to cry again.

Suddenly the sound of rowdy Roman soldiers coming down the dismal steps to the dungeon interrupted his anguish. The rats began to scramble into hiding as the heavy key began to clang in the lock. When the old door swung open the torches sent the last of the rats into their holes and caused the prisoners to swear and cover their eyes from the glare. A number of Lo-asah's comrades muttered as the seven guards moved across the filthy floor, kicking legs and filth out of their way as they went. The Romans shone the torches in the straining eyes of each man until their captain acknowledged, "Yes, he's one of them. And this one here, I believe he's the other rabble who attacked the garrison of Tiberias," he said as he poked a spear into Lo-asah's groin.

Lo-asah moaned and tried to cover his eyes from the pain of the light. Rough Roman hands began to unchain him from the wall as a soldier leaned him over on his side and put a knee in his ribs for leverage against the chains. Shemuel began to curse violently at the treatment and Lo-asah echoed him, since it seemed the thing to do. Suddenly a guard kicked him, in the mouth. "Curse Rome, will you?" And Lo-asah felt the foot again, snapping his head back against the stone wall. "You and your worthless people!" the Roman spat.

The blood trickled from Lo-asah's numb lip onto his beard as the two guards hurled him to his feet. Because of the leather bindings he had not been able to completely straighten his legs out for nearly two weeks, so he staggered feebly as they pushed him across the dungeon floor. Just in front of the door he tripped over another prisoner's feet, and the man spit on him and swore as the soldiers prodded Lo-asah to get up again with their daggers. Lo-asah could feel and sense that Shemuel also was staggering behind him as they went out the door and began to struggle up the staircase.

The stairs were quite slippery, and even the soldiers fought to manage their footing as they ascended. After about 30 steps they came to a second door, which was not quite as large and imposing as the door to the cell. The captain took his whip handle and struck the old wood three times as he called out, "Open, we have the rabble under control." A heavy bar slid aside, and then the door opened. The full light of the early sunrise exploded down the shaft of the staircase and Lo-asah nearly fell back from it, as if it were a great wind. Suddenly a spear shaft sent him reeling into the guard room.

Stumbling, unable to catch himself because of the thongs that lashed his hands behind his back, he fell and slammed his face against the floor. The captain of the guard kicked him in the side and shouted, "Get up, dog! It seems that the governor desires some early-morning justice. Let us entertain his wishes with two pieces of Israel's manure this morning!" The Romans laughed as they forcefully led Shemuel and Lo-asah out of the fortress and through the narrow streets to the palace of the governor of Judea, prefect of Rome, Pontius Pilate.

For nearly four years Pilate had ruled over Jerusalem. He was corrupt and capricious, vulgar and cunning. Hating the Jews and Judea, he was determined to make a name for himself by subjugating the region even more thoroughly under Rome's heel so he could return to the Senate in triumph. Pilate reasoned that an assignment like Jerusalem could make or break a career, and he was not about to be broken by some dismal outpost filled with barbarians who acknowledged only one God. Pilate also believed in only one god—power—and he worshiped it well.

Whenever he could, he would send a report of another insurrection crushed back to Rome. Knowing it was to his advantage, he looked for every little event that he could use for political benefit. If a group of children would make too much noise in the street he would send in a band of soldiers "to dispel the disturbance and put down the rebellion before it had time to brew." The troops did not trust Pilate. They knew he was much too petty for their real world, but they were the extension of Rome and the empire was based on loyalty to its will. And so it was that a common, second-class thief named Lo-asah of Sepphoris found himself dragged before the Jerusalem prefect that early morning to be accused of high treason against Rome.

Part III

THE FAILURE

⁙

Back in the acrid darkness Lo-asah sat quietly, desperately trying to think. The morning's events were so incomprehensible that he felt as if a boulder were crushing the life out of him. The dank air of the dungeon was even more oppressive as he struggled to breathe through the waves of horror that rolled over him. Everything seemed confused and disjointed. His rote trial had been short and pointless. Rome's concept of justice for a noncitizen was notorious throughout the empire, and Lo-asah quickly realized that to the empire he was but a gnat to be swatted in frustration.

It seemed that Pontius Pilate was feeling political pressure from Rome and needed more object lessons to intimidate the seething populace. After nearly four years he was having no greater success than any of his predecessors at bringing Judea into submission. The emperor wanted peace, and Pilate wanted whatever the emperor desired. The Senate had not come up with any new solutions to the problem of Judea, and they certainly were not going to expend any more resources on it. The previous night, at a banquet to honor a retiring legionary commander, a legate from Rome had made it clear that the patience of the emperor, the consuls, and the Senate had just about reached an end. The Jews had to be brought to subjugation, and if Pilate was not capable of accomplishing it, then someone would be found who could.

The governor's career and dreams lay in the fate of Judea. Therefore he determined to use every possible event to his benefit. Pilate decided that he would bribe, threaten, punish, cajole, and manipulate every Jew until he accomplished his

The Failure

purpose. Following the banquet the odor of the spices and meats had not yet dissipated before Pilate set about his task with a new energy. He would establish his name in Judea, and Lo-asah and Shemuel just happened to have the poor judgment of choosing to commit a minor crime at exactly the wrong time. He would demonstrate his complete authority in the presence of the masses who had come to Jerusalem for the Passover and for the legate before he sailed with the first spring breezes.

Lo-asah still remembered Pilate's disdain and anger that morning. "You Jews are more trouble than you are worth in the empire. Rome, in generosity, protects you and brings you stability, and to what purpose? You all run roughshod in the streets. You scamper in the mountainsides as wild animals without a mother. Your massive Temple runs with the blood of your sacrifices to your antiquated God." The prefect stood and spit out his frustration. "We rule the world, and you seem to forget that your David has been in his grave for a thousand years. When will you recognize that Solomon is not returning to lead you in splendor? Your day is past. It is a Roman world, and you will either learn to live in it or you will be crushed beneath our feet, just as we have so destroyed all other pretenders to power."

Lo-asah did not understand the implications of the governor's tirade at first. He was not politically sensitive enough to realize that he was going to become an expendable playing piece in a much larger game. When they first entered the stark judgment hall Lo-asah expected another serious beating, some public humiliation, and then a sentence in the quarries of Seir. But when Pilate made his final pronouncement it seemed as though all the color faded from the robes and judgment seat and standards of the guard. Lo-asah felt as though every fiber of his body exploded when Pilate spoke, in measured terms, "I pronounce you fit for only one conclusion. You shall be crucified for the benefit of Rome."

The prefect sneered at the two condemned men as he turned and left the room. Crucified! It couldn't be! Not for such a petty crime as stealing a bridle. Crucified!

Lo-asah had seen crucifixion. All Jews had witnessed the form of execution. It was a revolting and nauseous death. The slow wasting of a naked victim in the elements was the nightmare that Rome had perfected to terrorize populations into submission. A crucified person might die in several ways. Some expired from the exposure to hot days and long cold nights that sapped away at a failing body. Others died a heinous death as ants and other vermin crawled into the nose and ears and wounds and slowly ate the victim alive. Some victims choked to death in their own blood as their lungs tore when they struggled to fight against the increasing paralysis of their chest muscles while they hung on a cross. Still others suffered a lingering death from the incredible damage done by an impaling spike that tore into the torso between the legs. The signs of internal hemorrhage (such as raging thirst) were often quite common at crucifixions.

Crucified! The word exploded in Lo-asah's mind over and over as he finally sobbed in the darkness. He never would have guessed that it could come to that conclusion. The young nephew of Zadok the would-be Pharisee bitterly recounted the choices and semi-choices of his life. What weighed down his heart all the more was the fact that there had been more "semi"-choices than choices. He had always been only a follower. Never, even in his childhood mischief, had he ever instigated anything. He always went down the path of least resistance, and now he discovered to his horror that it stopped at a cross. It was never supposed to end like that.

Lo-asah always assumed that someday he would stand for some noble cause. He always felt that he was destined to make his mother proud of him and that he would bring honor to his father's name. But that was not what Rome had in mind—to them he was only a condemned man whose name had not even been spoken at his trial. He could not bear to think of his mother. She would surely never mention his name again and would go to her grave in anguish, without the comfort of the community for her grief.

The Failure

And what did God think? He'd already made His intentions known. "Cursed be he who hangs on a tree . . ." Lo-asah's heart shattered. Only numbness enabled him to endure the hours following the trial.

That night he wished that the Romans had killed him immediately, but that would not have served their purpose. The goal of crucifixion was to humiliate, degrade, and terrorize. For even a relative to show any grief over its victim was to instantly invite crucifixion for the whole family. The bodies could not be buried but must hang in public disgrace. It was a family shame to a Jew to leave a body unburied. Pilate was saving him and Shemuel as object lessons for the pilgrims that would soon converge on Jerusalem. The guards knew the time scheduled for his execution, but they would not tell. The idea was for the condemned prisoner to suffer every minute until death would finally release him.

Days dragged by in the dungeon, and Lo-asah found himself being alternately swept by fear, anger, horror, rage, and despair. Only fitful sleep would deliver him at times from the void that eventually developed where his heart had once been. Shemuel would randomly begin to scream and swear, and so Lo-asah, again out of long habit, would echo the obscenities, but they never made sense. Curses did nothing to change the horrifying facts. He was going to die a senseless death and bring to an end a rather senseless life. It was not supposed to end like that. His mother had dreamed of him becoming a Pharisee, and now Rome would use him as an example of its cruel power.

Crucifixions were always public events to increase the terror. Few argued the deterrent factor of a punishment in which a victim would linger for up to two weeks by the side of the main highway north of the city. Pilate understood well that if he showed no deference to the Jewish festival and was willing to crucify during its sacred hours, it demonstrated that he cared little for public opinion. The word of his determination would spread across the map as the masses of pilgrims returned to their various lands carrying the memory of still another Roman execution.

Thirty-five years earlier Herod had had the whole leadership of the Sanhedrin executed by crucifixion. It seemed that five young men had climbed up the Temple wall at night to knock down the imperial Roman eagle mounted over the eastern gate. Herod captured the young revolutionaries and had them burned alive at Caesarea in Philippi. To teach his subjects a lesson he took all of the Jerusalem leadership to the cross. That was the way that Rome and its servants dealt with problems. It was rumored that once Rome put down a slave revolt by crucifying its participants along the major highway into Rome from the sea. A distance of 60 miles, it provided enough space to crucify 20,000 slaves. The deterrent factor must have worked, for many years went by before the slaves rebelled again.

Crucifixions had taken place in Sepphoris. At times the garrison at Tiberias would stage executions by the city gate to remind the people of the Galilee that Rome's will was preeminent. Few in Palestine hadn't seen crucifixion at one time or another. The Passover provided the perfect opportunity to provide the visual lesson of power to others from lands less rebellious than Judea. As Lo-asah awaited his execution he realized that he would die a nameless victim, just an object lesson. "Cursed be he who hangs on a tree. . . ."

After an unknown number of days the sound of footsteps stirred the prisoners in the rotten cell. It was evident by the noise and crude banter of the soldiers that it was not just mealtime. The heavy key turned in the old lock and the door swung open abruptly, flooding the blackness with the brilliance of the torches. The captain of the guard commanded, "There, over there, take that one and the one next to him there!"

Lo-asah's hands covered his burning eyes, but he sensed that he was one of the chosen. He heard the footsteps approach his position, and then rough hands grabbed at his bindings and began to release him from the wall. Shemuel began to scream, "No, no, I don't want to die! No!" The calloused hands forced a pole beneath Lo-asah's arms as his hands remained bound. The soldiers ripped him to his feet and forced him ahead on his

The Failure

unsteady legs. As he neared the door he could sense that Shemuel was struggling against the guard, so Lo-asah began to imitate him. His attempt at escape lasted for only a brief moment as he felt the jailer bring the heavy ring of keys down on the side of his head, staggering him to his knees. The ringing in his ear drowned out the curses of the soldiers, and he barely sensed that he was being forced up the slimy stairs into the light of the room above and then out through the doorway.

When Lo-asah's mind began to clear he struggled to look around and saw a great number of soldiers gathered in a courtyard. Milling around, they laughed with anticipation yet acted nervous in their bravado. Shemuel stood a bit to his left, and when Lo-asah was able to focus on him he saw that his comrade looked terrible. His hair and beard were filthy and matted, and what was left of his garments was shredded. Lo-asah realized that he probably presented the same appearance and closed his eyes, for he did not want to see any more.

Just then he heard a commotion on the far side of the courtyard. A large contingent of soldiers marched through the old gate, dragging a Prisoner with them. Lo-asah opened his eyes to see what was going to happen and nearly retched as he saw the Man. The flesh was shredded on the Man's torso. Large flies crawled in the open wounds and the Man, nearly naked, was oblivious to them. Suddenly one soldier, a particularly ugly individual, cleared his throat deeply and spit directly in the Prisoner's face. Several other guards laughed and began to imitate Him. Just then Lo-asah felt a soldier spitting on him, and he knew he had never understood such shame.

The new Prisoner had a circle of thorns rammed on His head, and the soldiers forced the spines into His scalp by hitting them with small sticks. Lo-asah saw the Man stagger for a moment and collapse to His knees. One of the guards quickly kicked a swift blow to the Prisoner's mouth and nose and knocked Him backward. Three other soldiers roughly forced the Prisoner to His feet and then untied His hands. Another soldier brought a wooden beam over from a stack near the wall and threw it onto the Prisoner's shoulder. The Man wobbled under the weight as the executioners adjusted the beam so that the majority of the weight was off the back. That would require the Man to carry it leaning forward because He could not balance it if He stood upright.

Lo-asah then felt a guard cutting his bindings, and another laid a crossbeam upon his shoulder. The splinters dug into his flesh as they also adjusted the beam off-balance for him. Instinctively Lo-asah leaned forward to keep from falling backward. His hands were lashed over the top of the beam, and he felt a spear point in his back as a soldier shouted, "On then, Judean dogs! Let us go feed the ants!"

The soldiers laughed as the procession began to move out of the courtyard. Lo-asah saw Shemuel at the head of the group and then the Stranger was forced into the line, with Lo-asah trailing. When the huge gate swung open Lo-asah was suddenly stunned. The roar of a huge crowd exploded through the opening. Hundreds of people shrieked and swore. He struggled to look past his arm and through his filthy hair hanging over his eyes. Something seemed to be extremely wrong.

Questions exploded in his mind. Why were there so many to witness his execution? He was only a common thief. Why were people hanging from buildings and rooftops to catch a glimpse of the serpentine precession? Why were there Temple priests, in full regalia, following the Roman guards through the crowd? Why did some spit as the victims passed, while others looked as if they were fighting back anguish lest the Romans see them and execute them for showing sympathy? What was happening? It was all beyond him.

The crush of the crowd made passage difficult through the narrow street. Guards were swearing and forcing the populace against the walls to clear the way. After an abrupt turn in the old city street the procession came to a stairway. Lo-asah tripped and fell on one of the first steps. Unable to bring his hands down from the top of the beam, he fell on his face on the step above. He felt several teeth break and struggled to his feet as a Roman kicked him in the side and screamed, "Get up, you filth; this is no time to rest! You'll have plenty of time to relax when we hang you up. On now!" And Lo-asah spit blood as he staggered under the load again.

After several long minutes Lo-asah realized that the procession was barely making progress, for the third Man kept falling on His face and elbows. When the guard rolled Him over, Lo-asah saw that the Stranger's elbows were bloodied and shattered, split open from the paving stones. Eventually, in frustration, the Roman commander grabbed a man from the crowd and forced the beam on his back. The man complained bitterly until a heavy Roman hand slapped him across the mouth and then shoved him on up the narrow street. Another guard kicked the third condemned man in the groin and left him writhing on the ground.

Suddenly a young woman broke from the crowd and knelt beside the Stranger. She pulled at the skirt of her robe and began, struggling through her tears, to wipe the blood and the filth from His face. Lo-asah recognized her. It was one of the prostitutes of Magdala. He had known her and used her services several times. Magdala was notorious, for it was the village closest to the Tiberias garrison. Many women of ill-repute plied their trade in that village, since business often was good after the troops were paid. At times Lo-asah had also sought the company of one of the women of Magdala.

Why would a prostitute of Magdala be weeping and nursing the wounds of this Man? After a moment one of the soldiers grabbed her unceremoniously and shouted, "Be gone, whore! This man doesn't need your services now." He hurled her against the wall. Why didn't they drag her off for instant crucifixion? Then two other soldiers grabbed the condemned Man and rolled Him over to force Him to His feet.

It was in that moment that Lo-asah first saw the Man's face clearly. He was stunned—he had seen Him before. It was in Galilee some months before. Simon's band had gone toward the lake to raid some storehouses in Capernaum and pleasure

127

themselves in Magdala. As they passed by a small village they noticed quite a crowd gathered near the town spring. Simon suggested that they might be able to pass through the assembly and find some treasure that was not being guarded well. When Lo-asah came to the center of the crowd he discovered that the gathering seemed to have assembled around one Man. It was the Prisoner, sitting with several children on His knee. The children were laughing with Him as He had just whispered something into their ears that seemed to be a secret. Mothers and old men smiled as they observed the scene.

For a moment Lo-asah paused to watch when suddenly the Man spoke. He began a story that fascinated Lo-asah. Lo-asah felt himself strangely drawn to the Man as he listened. Mesmerized by the tale, for a brief time he forgot his banditry. The Man was teaching about God and spiritual things, but His words seemed so unlike the pompous and cold authority of Zadok and the synagogue elders. Then, as quickly as it had begun, the moment was over. One of Simon's band grabbed Lo-asah's robe and said boisterously, "Come, let us go. There's nothing for our kind here. Besides, Magdala awaits!"

That day as he walked away from the crowd he felt a distinct sadness in his heart. Magdala's pleasures were a great disappointment that night as he found himself haunted by the Man's stories. Neither the prostitute nor the wine could erase the ringing words of the Teacher by the lake. But again the moment passed, and Lo-asah soon thought little of the event until he glimpsed the Man lying on the street in Jerusalem. Suddenly a great sadness overwhelmed his own pain and humiliation. It truly was an evil world. Scum, like himself, deserved whatever they got. But if the world could not provide a place for a Man like the Teacher, then perhaps it all didn't matter anyway. It really shouldn't end that way, at least not for someone like the storyteller.

Part IV

THE FAILURE

°°
°

L o-asah painfully returned to the present when a young man from the crowd hit him on the left ear with a broken piece of pottery. For a moment he lurched to respond, but a soldier intervened with the handle of a whip pointed directly at his throat and shouted, "On now, you scum; you have rested long enough. You have an appointment with the vultures who wish to scrape out your eyes. Move!" And with that he pushed Lo-asah on down the street to his destiny.

In the confusion of screaming, oaths, and tears, the intensity of the moment caused the short journey to the outside of the wall to stretch interminably. Lo-asah's ears rang, and he eventually found himself becoming dizzy and nauseous from the press of the crowd and the pain of the splinters digging into his neck and shoulders. Just before the procession exited the Damascus gate a bitter old woman spit on him and stuck out her walking rod to trip him up. Lo-asah stumbled for a few steps, and just as he thought he had caught his balance, the soldier behind gave him another shove, sending him falling forward under the heavy beam. Unable to catch himself because of the bindings on his hands, he instinctively turned his head to avoid taking the full blow of the cobblestone directly on his face. But unexpectedly something stopped him from falling completely and splitting open his elbows on the stones. Lo-asah heard a scream, and the guard rolled him over. He opened his eyes to see a soldier swearing at him and preparing to lash him for his clumsiness.

"Don't you care for anything, dog? Look what you've done to this child!" The guard ripped Lo-asah's matted hair from his eyes, and he saw a small girl lying stunned on the pavement. The child could not have been more than 4 years old. A growing stream of blood oozing from just above her ear dampened her hair. The crossbeam apparently had struck the child on its way down. Lo-asah was overwhelmed with anguish at what he had caused. When the young mother began to wail, clutching her child, Lo-asah suddenly rolled over and vomited. Some of it splattered the guard's legs and sandals.

The soldier went insane. He screamed and swore and began to violently beat Lo-asah around the head and neck. With his hands lashed over the beam, Lo-asah was unable to defend himself from any of the blows. The crowd drew back in horror as some of them began to be sprayed by blood and vomit. The beating continued until the captain of the guard intervened. "Off him, Lucius! I order you to stop! If you kill him here, we will only have a worthless carcass to nail up." Several other soldiers ran to separate them as the captain continued, "Now, force him up. Come, you filth, up to your feet now!"

The soldiers grabbed his arms and jerked him violently to his feet, reset the crossbeam, and pushed the condemned man on his way.

Once the procession left the narrow streets as they exited the northern gate, the mob had more room to spread out. It would have seemed that there should be some release from the press of the crowd, but if anything more people waited outside the wall. Through his pain and shock Lo-asah struggled to understand why so many had come to watch the event. One of the men who stood by the side, quite obviously a foreigner by dress and accent, had shouted, "So this is how you Romans respect our Passover? You desecrate everything you touch!" In the darkness of the cell Lo-asah had quite lost track of time. He had forgotten it was time for the celebration. Still, just because of the mass of Jews who returned in pilgrim faithfulness for the observance, it didn't seem logical that so many would be interested in witnessing another execution. If anything, it would have seemed that they would want to avoid the pollution of such an event of the eve of the holy day.

Lo-asah easily determined that the mob had little interest in Shemuel's death—and certainly not in his. Instinctively, he knew that the execution of the Teacher was somehow drawing the multitude. The whole way he had heard Shemuel screaming above the din of the crowd. At times he found himself swearing at everyone—soldiers, taunting priests, old women silently waiting by the side of the road. But none of it made any sense, and the words would soon die in his parched throat.

But Lo-asah dimly realized that the Teacher, except for a deep groan one time, never uttered a sound. The rich voice that told such wonderful stories was silent. When Lo-asah considered it, he did not feel like swearing anymore. The other Prisoner's majestic silence overwhelmed Lo-asah, and he went the final distance to the crossroads without speaking also.

The serpentine mass of humanity finally reached the main juncture on the north side of town. A turn to the right would send a person toward Damascus, and the left road would end at the sea. At the base of the hill behind the road's fork Lo-asah could see the Roman uprights—the center poles for the crucifixions. Rome had perfected its art and had long ago discovered that leaving the center beams in place not only speeded up the executions, but acted as stark reminders of the potential of crucifixion and therefore also assisted in deterring future rebellious acts. The naked uprights constantly reminded the empire's subjects of the price they would have to pay for disloyalty.

As the prisoners approached the uprights, Lo-asah began to panic. He heard Shemuel begin to scream about how Simon would deliver him and make the Romans pay for their cruelty. His friend swore and kicked and struggled to break free. Lo-asah also realized that if he didn't escape now there would never be any possibility. Once a man was on a cross he was all but dead.

One time a band of revolutionaries in a village in Syria had sought to release a man from a cross. The local legion captured them all and crucified every one of them after forcing them to watch the full penalty of their crime. The Romans had slowly tortured every third man, woman, and child in the town to death before their eyes. Such object lessons taught well the will of Rome. Lo-asah knew that Simon was not coming. He knew there would be no deliverance once he was attached to his cross. Just as the soldiers ripped the crossbeam from his shoulders he began to thrash and struggle in a last desperate attempt to attain freedom. Then for a moment everything went numb.

When he regained consciousness he felt the blood flowing down over his ear from the blow of the butt end of the spear that had brought him to submission. On his knees, he opened his eyes to see the crimson puddle developing in the dust by his right leg. He struggled to stand but was thrown down upon his back. Just then a heavy Roman knee slammed into his stomach and knocked his breath away. Lo-asah was fighting for breath and had no strength to attempt to wrestle away from the one guard who stood on his left arm. Another soldier ripped Lo-asah's clothes off. A third soldier was wrapping his right hand, much too tightly, to the crossbeam. When he was done tying the knots he stood to step over Lo-asah to bind the left arm, but he paused above the young man for a moment and roared as he urinated on him. It was all part of the shame. It taught well the lessons of Rome.

The soldier stepped over to bind the left arm. When they had his wrist securely cinched up to the splintered wood, the three soldiers dragged the beam and the man over the rough ground and rocks to where the uprights had been removed from their holes. Lo-asah was thrown down on top of the post and the two pieces lashed together at the top of the center beam. A notch allowed the cross span to slide onto the upright. In horror Lo-asah felt the impaling spike between his legs. Not all crosses had a spike, but Lo-asah had seen the agony of those men who had died on crosses equipped with one. The force of the cross being thrown into its hole would slam the victim down on the spike and destroy their crotch and groin. It was a terrible sight.

The Failure

In the darkness of his cell in the last weeks before that day Lo-asah had prayed that he would not have a cross with a spike. It seemed, again, that God did not care about his life or his death. Lo-asah swore loudly at God as he felt his cross rise into the air. His curses became a screaming conclusion as the soldiers thrust the center beam down into the hole.

The pain and shock of the impaling seared through his body, and for quite a while Lo-asah was unconscious. During those moments when he was lucid he caught glimpses of the scene around him. He saw the Teacher quietly enduring the humiliation . . . the priests defiling themselves . . . Shemuel's horrifying scream as his cross dropped . . . the young Teacher's struggled breathing . . . the band of women and old men trying to hide their grief lest they be crucified also . . . the soldiers arguing over a large garment. . . the tearless, nearly sightless eyes of one older woman who stood at the base of the center cross and leaned on a young man for strength . . . Was it the Teacher's mother? Was she watching her son die?

Lo-asah thought of his own mother. By now the word must surely have reached Sepphoris about his fate, and he could imagine his mother gently rocking back and forth on her floor mat in the darkness. When he looked at the woman by the center cross he was glad that his mother was not in Jerusalem to witness this. Maybe God had done him one favor.

But he also knew his mother would never mention his name again. Whether it took four days or two weeks, Lo-asah knew that when he finally succumbed to death's deliverance, his mother would never speak his name again. In Sepphoris there would be no memorial for him. He had also surrendered any hope that Simon would ever propose a drink in his honor. The Romans would finally cast whatever might remain of his rotted body into the smoldering garbage pit of Hinnom on the south side of Jerusalem along with the Temple manure and city's waste and refuse. Lo-asah knew that his life was coming to nothing and that he was going to be erased from human memory. The anguish of his failure was overwhelming, and only the onset of another wave of pain delivered him temporarily from his thoughts.

Pain washed over Lo-asah's body in waves, building to an intensity that overwhelmed his nerves so that all sensation shut down. When he could feel, his thoughts were jumbled and disjointed, but when the numbness set in, he succumbed to a certain dreaminess—more like a dim and struggling nightmare. In one of his more lucid moments Lo-asah heard the taunting of a priest to the Teacher. "Some deliverer you turned out to be. Some Messiah! You can't even deliver yourself! If you're the Promised One, you must reveal it now to dispel our doubts."

The other priests, who stood in ceremonial robes, picked up the theme and began to vow, "Yes, if you now prove yourself to us, we will gladly follow you! Reveal yourself now, messiah! Deliver yourself, and we will march behind you in your triumph . . ." But the Teacher just bit His lip and closed His eyes as the holy ones waved their hands in disgust toward Him and turned away.

Lo-asah struggled through his dripping sweat to see what was written above the Teacher's head. He found that he could decipher only one of the three lines: "Jesus of Nazareth, King of Jews." He guessed the other two lines were in other languages. King of Jews, ha! For a while Shemuel had been taunting everyone in sight. Finally he told the priests what he thought of them, and the soldiers got what they deserved too. Even the watching women were not immune from his poison.

Without thinking Lo-asah found himself falling into the old and natural patterns, and he swore too. He cursed Rome, and the Temple, and the righteous Pharisees, and the God who never listened, and then he turned to curse Jewish kings who were powerless. . . .

But the words died when he saw the third crucifixion victim look toward the sky and groan, "It is all right, Father. Please forgive them. None of them know what they are doing. . . ."

How could He say that? The Teacher's gentle prayer took all the venom out of Lo-asah's bitterness and left him completely

The Failure

empty. He lapsed into silence until another wave of pain struck and swept him into semiconsciousness for a few minutes.

When he started to drift back into awareness, he heard Shemuel cursing again. Something inside of Lo-asah snapped and he screamed at him, "What is the matter with you? Don't you have one shred of decency in your miserable soul? You and I deserve this and more, but how dare you curse this man? He's done nothing! A man like this deserves to live. If there's a God in the heavens, this man deserves to live!"

Stunned, Shemuel became silent. The outburst took the crowd by surprise, and for a moment all eyes stared at Lo-asah in his nakedness and shame. But the Teacher also looked at him. Through His pain the eyes revealed a gentle gratitude. Lo-asah suddenly, without warning, without time for reason, said quietly, "Teacher, if ever there would be a kingdom, You would deserve to rule in it. Would You please remember me when You establish such a kingdom? I'd like to die believing that someone would think of me gently someday. . . ."

In the silence of the moment the Teacher's strong, rich voice cut through the pain and darkness and emptiness. For a moment He seemed bigger than the cross, larger than the events, more majestic than any king on earth. For a brief moment the young Teacher transcended all of it as He stated distinctly, "My friend, this day I swear to you, Paradise is yours."*

A strange and unexplainable warmth filled Lo-asah's being. His pain and guilt and shame no longer seemed to matter. He could not fully comprehend exactly what he had heard, but he knew he could die in peace. The Teacher gently smiled and then dropped His head back against the crossbeam as the pain once more shrouded Him. The rabble again fell to taunting. But for Lo-asah the whole universe was different.

---

*Some argue over the correct placement of the comma in the KJV statement "Verily I say unto thee, To day thou shalt be with me in paradise" (Luke 23:43). This discussion revolves around the Christian's concept about death. To those who believe in the nonimmortality of the soul and that death is only an absolute and unconscious sleep, the comma placement is vital. They claim that the added punctuation (which was not part of the original Greek text) is incorrect in this passage, that it was placed in that position because of the particular theological bent of the translator who worked on the passage. It is true that ". . ., To day . . ." is decidedly different from ". . . today, . . . "

I wish us to consider both sides for a moment, and then I will propose that it is perhaps not really the issue in the passage anyway.

If you choose to believe that Jesus intended "I say unto thee, today thou shalt be with me in paradise," you run up against three major problems.

1. It seems a terrible contradiction to the verses that state plainly that death is only an oblivious, nonexistent state compared to sleep (see Eccl. 9:5, 6, 7; Ps. 146:4; and more).

2. It changes Jesus' own perception about death from His previous statements to people such as Mary, Martha, and Jairus (John 11:11, 14, 15; Mark 5:35-42) .

3. Worst of all, it seems to make Jesus into a liar in three ways:

a. He previously told His disciples He would be in the grave for three days, not in paradise (Matt. 12:40).

b. He knew, and Lo-asah knew, that the two men on the crosses around Him were not going to, and did not, die that day (John 19:31-34). That's what crucifixion was all about. A quick, one-day death did not serve the empire's purpose of instilling terror in its subject peoples. At the event itself Lo-asah could not have misunderstood the time frame of Jesus' assurance to him.

c. At the poignant scene of the garden tomb Jesus expressed clearly to His grieving friend that He had not yet ascended to paradise (John 20:15-17). Would Jesus lie to Lo-asah? Or had He lied to the disciples? Or did He lie to Mary at the tomb? Or is there another way to view His statement of assurance?

But the problem is the comma. Some find an easy solution around what appears to be the contradiction of the placement of the punctuation and their belief that death is only an unconscious, totally oblivious, nonexistent interlude between this life and the day of resurrection at the end of time. They say, "move the comma!"

That creates several dilemmas. Some would argue that you have no right to do anything like that to Scripture. Even though the punctuation was not part of the original text and was a later addition to assist in clarification (just as chapterization also was), Scripture warns against adjusting its teachings to personal whim or bent. If I want to move the comma I will certainly have some who will quickly remind me of Jesus' words "one jot or one tittle shall in no wise pass from the law" (Matt. 5:18), or that the apostle John speaks against adding or subtracting from the Word (Rev. 22:18, 19), or that Paul said there is a correct and an incorrect way of "dividing the word of truth" (2 Tim. 2:15).

I might personally find those arguments inappropriate, or not applicable

The Failure

in the case of punctuation. But I submit that the whole dilemma is not necessary and the arguments are irrelevant. I ask you to consider that the comma can stay right where it is and still agree with the doctrine of soul sleep.

For Lo-asah, a secure eternity began that day. Paradise began in the heart of the failure (consider Acts 2:21, 32-36). Death, for all, may be an interruption, but it is not the end. The promise of Jesus is that whoever believes has eternal life. The money is in the bank. For a period of time you may not hold the cash in your hands, but it is still your money. Over the weekend, or on Christmas Day, you may not have access to the full reserve of your savings, but it is *your* money.

To every repentant soul eternity has already begun. Death may interrupt it, but then the reality is that the very best of this life is not even a dim foreshadowing of real living. "It doth not yet appear what we shall be" (1 John 3:2), and "Now we see through the glass, darkly" (1 Cor. 13:12), and "Eye hath not seen, nor ear heard, neither have entered into the heart of man, the things which God hath prepared for them that love him" (1 Cor. 2:9). Apparently, this life is not real living anyway.

We can permit Lo-asah to start Paradise that day even though he didn't die that day!

Part V

THE FAILURE

The waves of pain and nausea rushed over Lo-asah again, but they could not completely overcome the incredible peace and relief that he felt. It was as though in a moment, with one sentence, the young Teacher had filled the horrible, lifelong void in his heart. For the first time in his painful existence it seemed as though the war inside him was over. Lo-asah thought that if there was a God in the heavens He would certainly be like that Teacher. Through his intense pain he knew, somehow, that he was at peace with God. He would not die a forgotten man. The young thief smiled to himself until the pain engulfed him again.

As the afternoon dragged on Lo-asah became aware of an intense darkness settling over the land. It seemed as though heaven was no longer going to allow evil human beings to witness the Teacher's shame. For a moment it seemed that a great Father was shrouding His Son from those who would harm Him. The Temple priests and scribes began to grow uncomfortable, almost as though they had a premonition of some coming cataclysmic event. Some of the mob began to slip away quickly as if afraid of some sudden and unexpected catastrophe. Little clusters of women and children began to press together, and some appeared to have trouble breathing. The Roman guards whispered among themselves, their hands firmly on their weapons. Soon one of the older soldiers began to shout to the others that they should, perhaps, consider dispersing the crowd.

Then, without warning, the crucified Teacher whispered something through the desolation. Lo-asah heard part of the ancient psalm that had served as his childhood bedtime prayer

The Failure

also: "Father, into thy hands . . ." At the conclusion of the prayer it was as though the Man suddenly transcended the pain as He strained against the nails and impaling spike. He held His wounded head high and shouted up through the oppressing darkness, "I have finished!"

The Teacher's mutilated body strained with the words for a few seconds and then fell limp against the cross. For a moment a terrible silence hung over the scene. Suddenly the ground began to shake. People began to run, screaming.

Asah—for that is how he now somehow thought of himself, as one at last "filled"—felt the cross shake. He snapped his head as he strained to see through the swirling wind and dust. Shemuel also was struggling, but the Teacher's body hung limp and defeated, quietly resting against the cross despite the jolting of the earthquake.

Then, just as unexpectedly, another eerie silence fell around the execution site. The Roman captain, speaking to no one in particular, commented about the gods or something to that effect. Some of the priests began to argue with the captain of the guard. One of them pointed at the western horizon and then gestured toward the crosses. After a period of negotiation the captain turned to his men and shouted, "All right, you men, prepare to take them down. Our *hosts* do not want them on view over their Sabbath. Quickly now, let's get them off, but make sure they do not escape."

One of the older soldiers ran and grabbed the large mallet that they had used to drive the supporting wedges into the base of the crosses. He then took it to Shemuel's cross and with one blow shattered Shemuel's left leg just below the knee. Shemuel screamed and swore as the soldier crushed his right leg.

He then handed the mallet to a younger soldier and said as he gestured toward the Teacher, "Here, Alexander, you try your hand on that one." The guard went to the center cross, but before he swung he looked up at the limp form. A troubled expression crossed his face, and he turned to his superior officer and said, "Sir, I believe this man is dead."

139

The more experienced soldier ran forward and replied, "Dead? He can't be dead! I've participated in dozens of executions and no one dies that quickly. Here, Marcus, bring your spear and see if he's dead." One of the other soldiers stepped forward and began to prod the Teacher to see if there would be any response or reflex action. The body remained motionless.

Finally, in frustration, the scarred veteran roughly grabbed the shaft and thrust it in deep under the bloody ribs. The soldier with the mallet lurched backward and fell as a stream of blood and body fluids sprayed him. The older soldier laughed roughly, "Well, Alexander, it seems he is dead!" The veteran continued to laugh as he helped his companion to his feet.

The older man then took the mallet and approached the base of Asah's cross. He struggled but could not escape the blow. Pain seared in his left knee and then a moment later an echoing flash came from his right leg. Asah began to heave involuntarily. It did not seem possible that his body was capable of any more pain, but his shattered legs screamed through his numbness. Explosions of light flashed before his eyes when he dimly felt rough hands struggling against the knots that bound him to the cross. He struggled to see as they lowered him almost to the ground. Then, just before he was settled on a litter, one of the soldiers lost his grip and the others just released the limp burden. Asah collapsed by the side of the litter, every fiber of his body in agony.

The older soldier hooked his foot under Asah's arm and flipped him unceremoniously over onto the litter. Asah, for a moment, flashed in and out of awareness as he felt himself being lifted. Opening his eyes, he saw the captain of the guard standing near him. He wanted to lift himself but found that dropping the cross into its hole had dislocated his shoulders. The pain would not allow him to push himself up against the restraints. In desperation Asah called out, "Captain, does Rome allow a dying man a request?"

"What do you want, Jew?"

"Please, sir, could I see the man on that cross more closely?"

The Failure

The captain paused for a moment, glanced toward the setting sun, then finally said, "Be quick about it." Gesturing to the guards, he added, "Haul him over to the base of that cross, but only for a moment."

The soldier at the end of the litter by his feet swore under his breath as they turned and carried the broken criminal over by the center cross. Asah looked up at the lifeless form of the Teacher and began to cry. Struggling against the burning pain, he leaned up on one elbow to roll over. When he finally raised up on his side, Asah reached his hand out to try to brush some of the ants off of the blood that was already drying on the upright.

The hardened soldiers paused in unexpected silence at the scene for a moment, then one of them grew impatient. "Let's go," he said. "That's enough sentiment." The Roman shook the litter in a manner that rolled Asah back to its center. The guard shifted his grip and said, "Come now, let's carry this piece of vulture bait back to his hole. His rat friends are getting lonely!" The other soldiers laughed rudely, and they turned toward Jerusalem.

The return trip through the streets of the city took much less time than the journey out of the city had six hours before, as the streets seemed deserted. The faithful, in their homes, were oblivious to the passing band as they welcomed the Sabbath. Quickly the soldiers had the two crucifixion victims back in the fortress of Antonia and were bouncing their litters down the stairway to the lower dungeons. Once inside the heavy door, the guards dragged each litter to the far wall and rudely dumped its helpless load on the rotten straw. Then the room went dark as the door slammed shut.

The prisoners heard the fading steps and the receding voices laughing about their plans for the night and whether the wine would be wet enough to wash away the work of the day.

Finally, in the darkness a voice broke the measured breathing and soft moans of the two returned prisoners. "Lo-asah, is that you?"

"Yes," he struggled to answer. "Yes, I am back, Ephraim."

"I am afraid to ask because I don't think I really want to know . . . How is it? What is it like?"

"It is really horrible," he responded through clenched teeth as a sharp wave of pain swelled through his body. When the rolling explosion subsided a few minutes later, Asah whispered, "Ephraim, it is really bad, but I want to tell you about a man I just met out there . . ."

SPRING REPORT

⁚⁚

Marcus, captain of the Jerusalem Garrison, son of Malchus of Alexandria (by the hand of Gaius of Troas, scribe):

To Lucius Aurelius, honored commander of the Second Imperial Legion of Rome based in Judea. Trusted servant of Senate and Consul:

Hail, Lucius, in the name of all the gods and of Caesar, I honorably present my report of the recent activities and imperial involvement in the Jerusalem region. I trust, most noble Lucius, that this letter finds you well. I am confident that the salt breeze of Caesarea Maritima reminds you of your home at Puteoli. May you soon find such favor of the imperial hand that you may be reassigned to Italy. I know this is your desire also. As for myself, I would take the Syrian frontier over Judea. My two years here make me long for another post of service.

These Jews are a troublesome lot. The whole world, with minor and temporary exceptions, have accepted the destiny of Rome. Our enlightened occupation has brought civilization and culture to the far reaches of earth. Everywhere peace exists and the enemies of Rome have been vanquished. It seems that only Judea remains a constant irritant to the Senate and a concern to the emperor. Strangers, aliens (such as myself), have universally recognized the destiny of the gods in choosing a little village on the Tiber to sit as queen of the nations. All except for Judea. Though temporary rebellions rise throughout the realm, it is only this cursed spot (which these Jews call their "chosen land") that singularly remains disenfranchised. I grieve that our enlightened occupation has been met with such irrational resistance.

Last week I gratefully received your generous transfer of the 200 Gallic spearmen. These past six or seven weeks in Jerusalem have been most difficult.

You, in wisdom, warned me of the potential dangers of the patriotic backwash that seems always to accompany all Jewish festivals. We followed your counsel in preparing for the influx of pilgrims who returned to Jerusalem for their Passover celebration.

This was my second involvement with these Jews at this, their feast of independence from Egypt. We had the whole garrison on double alert, and I commanded that every man, in the name of Caesar, refrain from wine and frivolity for the duration of the feast. (If it were any but Hebrew wine I might have reconsidered, but this swill only serves to wash away the dust of Israel. Never shall Jewish wine make a man as does the wine of Italy, or even Syria, for all that matter.)

I am honored to report, most noble Aurelius, that the men of your command served well during a most difficult time. The city was astir with rumor. These Jews, and their barbaric "one God," seemed particularly intense this year. Their "messiah/deliverer" talk swept everywhere.

I am compelled to report that even Pontius Pilate and Herod of Galilee complicated our duty by their petty rivalry.

Approximately four days before the Passover festival the mob of Jerusalem became nearly unmanageable. It seemed that a seditious proclamation of a new king was being heralded in the Kidron Valley near Mount Olivet. A rabbi from Nazareth (a supposed magician) was riding a donkey as though a king triumphant. The mob seemed predisposed to recognize him as the legitimate heir of the throne of David of Jerusalem. I was ready to assemble the troops in the Antonia when representatives from the Temple class urged us to move slowly. They feared what might happen if we made a full show of Roman might at that time. The legates of the high priest assured me profusely and personally that they would control the matter without any need for Rome's help.

Spring Report

The events of the week proved their claim nonsense.

As the days progressed I knew I could no longer defer to their requests. The problem was bigger than just Jerusalem, for there were Jews (and those they call "God-fearers") from throughout the empire. The epidemic of restlessness could have spread if we did not take swift and appropriate action. Rome has not taught me to be indecisive, and as the days passed I knew I could not long allow the events to build any more lest they sweep all of us away.

I had heard this man on the donkey before, this Jesus. Once, perhaps twice, I had seen him teaching in the Temple. At first I never understood why his presence and teaching created such a great stir among the Jerusalem leadership. Yes, his ethic and teaching was absolutely opposed to the corruption rampant among the Temple group. But he was only one man, and they were so entrenched in their system that no single person could ever threaten them. I fully believed that.

But when I heard him speak I began to believe that this one man could shatter the world we know. And now, honored commander, I, at times, wonder if this one man wasn't a threat to even Rome herself. (I am amazed that I would even write or think of it). His teaching was simple, and the kingdom he spoke of, were it to exist, would find many citizens. If his God were real it would be a worthy God—but apparently a very jealous God who tolerates no competition. I always find this Jewish "one God" idea a primitive and barbaric necessity for a conquered people who still want to esteem themselves "chosen." But his "one God" seemed to be all-encompassing.

The kingdom of the itinerant rabbi attracted me (although the foundations of his kingdom were so contrary to Rome.) Imagine an empire based on love and justice. All rebellion would end, and I suppose that soldiers, such as you and I, would have to seek another occupation.

The jealous interplay of the body politic would cease. I am astounded that some of this finds positive response in me, but I guess that at this stage of my career fighting has lost its enchantment.

The Judean Chronicles

By the gods, I cannot believe that I am reporting this to you. But if I could not tell you this I could tell no one. You have served as inspiration and confidant—more father than superior. I trust you are not distressed at my honesty.

I assure you that none of this will affect the fulfillment of my duty to Rome or my duty to you. It did not seven weeks ago.

As we approached the eve preceding the Passover the Temple mercenaries rudely demanded my help in putting down a "rebellion." I sensed no insurrection—only great apprehension on the part of the priests and leadership. When I discovered that the Sanhedrin was in session, I demanded an explanation. Not only was that body convened without my permission but they were meeting at night, something contrary to their own laws. The whole event reeked of deception and subterfuge.

The leaders of Jerusalem gave feeble excuses about a supposed conspiracy against the Temple and against Roman authority. They claimed that it demanded their immediate attention. I let those "loyal" subjects know in no uncertain terms that Rome did not need their assistance, that I sensed no plot of rebellion and if there had been one, I would have dealt with it myself.

I would have dispersed them if Pilate had not requested I go along with them. As a soldier I am duty bound to assist the representatives of the Senate, but, most noble Lucius, I am afraid that I chafe under the task that puts my men at risk just to appease fat governors. Any such action only guarantees that someone will have to pay a price later. These small men are so short-sighted. They only want to climb another level up the ladder while we, the servants at risk, must constantly hold the empire's foundations together at the price of our blood.

And so, owing to the petty interplay of Pilate, Herod, and the Temple leadership, my men became involved in the crucifixion of Jesus of Nazareth and two common criminals whose names are not worth remembering.

I might interject here that Pilate, in all his wisdom, released from our custody Barabbas the insurrectionist. Again, I fear we

Spring Report

will pay for that in the future. I have had my belly full of minor governors and officials.

Through the long night of childish intrigue my men became increasingly tense. I sensed I had to release the pressure on them somehow, so when one of them asked if they could play "You Would Be King" with the prisoner, I acceded. I personally have always seen that drunken challenge as barbaric, and I rejoiced when the emperor banned it among the troops. As well you know, the imperial forces lost some capable leadership at the hand of lesser soldiers until we forbade that practice.

Normally I would have little problem with them doing it to a noncitizen prisoner. But I honestly wished my men had not chosen *that* prisoner. It was as though the men who had risked their lives for me became demons. I finally called a halt to the game and was horrified that they had shredded him so.

Through beaten and bloodied eyes he looked at me without hate. I felt as though I could not escape his gaze. Why did he not spit back? Why did he not murmur? Why did he not curse?

Eventually we took him to the cliffs outside the city wall at the juncture of the highway to Damascus.

Noble Aurelius, we have perfected crucifixion for the benefit of the empire and the will of the Senate, but now I am sickened of it. The cross has served the purpose of the gods, but I have never been so revolted by the brutality of it all as I was through the long hours of that day.

I found the whole scene repulsive. The vulgarity of my men, the pompous arrogance of the Jewish "holy men," the sickening curiosity of the crowd, the profane screams of the two other prisoners—all these things made me wish that I will never have to crucify anyone again.

Much to my surprise this one prisoner died quickly. (Some of me believed that a man of his kingdom could not die.) Oh, it is not that he died but the grace and acceptance of his own death that surprised me. He did not curse his God. Very quickly he shouted, "Finished!" and it was over. Immediately it seemed as though the gods mourned and nature turned capricious.

The Judean Chronicles

When I came to myself, I said, "This cannot be. What type of object lesson will this revolutionary be if he dies for Rome in only a day?" But he was very dead; I assure you of that.

Contrary to normal practice, I allowed his followers to have his body. Surely, a dead rebel leader cannot harm the eagle of Rome. (At least that is what I thought at the time.) In the middle of the night I was stirred from my quarters (I was not sleeping) by the insane command to have a portion of the garrison guard the tomb of the teacher. It seemed that Pilate must have been drunk on some lousy Jewish brew. But I am a soldier; I do my duty.

My men complained, but I commend them for their obedience. The hours of the Jewish Sabbath passed without incident. I sought Pilate to relieve my men of the ridiculous detail, but he refused to receive my emissary. From the fortress we witnessed a great deal of commotion and activity in the Temple court, in the western administrative wing, and on the path to the home of the high priest. This was rather unusual for their Sabbath, and I ordered the garrison on alert. At the time it seemed an appropriate, even prudent, response. I do not believe I overreacted to the situation.

The events of that night and the following early-morning hours are still unclear to me. I have men, battle-hardened and loyal to Rome, who swear that an explosion of light shattered the seal of his tomb. They claim they were paralyzed and observed the crucified prophet walk from his grave. I know this has been already reported to you. Most noble Lucius, I wish I could dispel this rumor, but I cannot.

I trust these men. They stared death in the face at Tramoni and confronted the suicide charge of the Parthian brigade at Pelaskartam. My men have laughed in the face of Hades many times for me. Walking the roads of Judea alone, they are prepared at any time to encounter Zealot bands. Yet I cannot comprehend the story they tell about that morning. They swear by the gods that he is alive again.

Numerous reports of his appearance have surfaced during

the past seven weeks. He has been "seen" in Jerusalem, Judea, throughout Galilee . . . We have heard of, and interrogated, hundreds who have "seen" him alive. They all tell the same story, and we do not seem to be capable of stopping it. Each of them genuinely believe him not to be dead any longer.

Just 10 days ago I received a report that he was walking through Jerusalem with a large crowd—perhaps more than 100 of His followers. I hurried to confront the "rumor," but it seems the apparition had exited the Eastern Gate before we arrived.

We hastened across the Kidron Valley, but before we reached the base of the hill, there seemed to be a commotion, a brightness, on the summit. Through the dense canopy of the olive trees we could not see clearly what was occurring, but when we broke into a clearing in the grove his followers were running down the path toward us. We readied ourselves for the assault, then saw that they were laughing, dancing, and praising their God.

"What do you mean by this assembly?" I demanded.

They shouted, "He is risen and now is ascended into heaven!"

I trust I did not fail you, my leader, but I allowed them to continue on to the city. It seemed, at the time, that no power, not even Rome, would silence them. I suppose time will tell of the will of the gods in this regard.

The past 10 days have been quiet enough, but we now face the festival they call Shabuoth or Pentecost. Again Jerusalem teems with the mass of the Jewish faithful from throughout the realm. Again we sense great expectation among the pilgrims. We may be in for more challenges.

I can only be honest with you. I don't know if that man is dead or alive. From what I have heard him say I almost wish he was alive. A man such as he deserves to live. I trust that I am not disloyal to my honored duty when I admit that his kingdom strikes a response in me.

But now, most honored Lucius, I must bring my report to a swift conclusion. It appears that the followers of Jesus are causing a commotion. One of them, Peter Bar-Jonas, apparently is stirring the crowd into a frenzy. My duty says I must stop this. Do trust that I will report on the outcome of this day to you.

My greetings to the command of Caesarea. Farewell, in the name of Caesar.

THE FIRST
GENERATION DIES

Statement of memory
for the death in Jerusalem of
Nicodemus Ben Jehuda
of the house of Malthace in Zipphorus of Galilee

The second day of the week past marked the death and burial of Nicodemus of Zipphorus. The man will be remembered in Jerusalem as a noted and notorious member of the aristocracy of Israel. His last years were controversial, and his death evoked mixed response from Jerusalem's leadership. This ambivalence results from the former Sanhedrin member's chosen allegiance to the followers of the crucified sect leader of Nazareth, Jesus.

Nicodemus (of memory) was born to prosperity and privilege as the eldest son of Jehuda of Zipphorus. Jehuda's wealth came from his alliance with the cause of Herod during the revolt against the Parthian occupation of Jerusalem some 85 years ago. Jehuda had an uncanny sense of the winds of providence and sought to align himself with Herod when the refugee king returned from Rome with the mandate of the Senate to subjugate Judea again for the empire of Caesar. During the subsequent three years of warfare, Jehuda's spice caravans provided funds to sustain Herod's 6,000 horsemen. That act ingrained him into the circle of privilege when Herod finally brought down the Persian banners in Jerusalem.

As a sign of gratitude, and a lesson to those who might consider opposing him, Herod granted Jehuda exclusive trade privileges on the Via Maris. Jehuda's wealth increased greatly through the passing years. Unlike other suitors, Jehuda managed to retain the favor of the Idumean king through all his various intrigues. Following one of Herod's insane tirades of crucifixion, Jehuda's only son, Nicodemus (of memory), was appointed to a vacancy of the Sanhedrin (which the king himself had created through violence). The young man had only attained the age of 22.

Nicodemus (of memory) remained in that position until his stunning resignation after the Shabuoth (Pentecost) festival uproar in the Temple court during the fourth year of the Roman prefect of Jerusalem, Pilate. Claiming allegiance to the sect of those who followed the cursed leader Jesus (may his name be stricken from memory), Nicodemus (of memory) broke all precedent for the body of the Sanhedrin by renouncing his rights. Never had any other member resigned his lifetime position before that fateful announcement.

(It may be noted that two other resignations from the court have occurred since Nicodemus (of memory) set a precedent for such a choice. Soon after he vacated his seat, another member, the scholar of Arimethea, Joseph Malchus, followed in Nicodemus' steps and also announced his resignation from the court because of allegiance to the condemned Nazarene sect. Then, three years later, the young prodigy of Gamaliel, Saul ben Dioklas of Cilesia (known now by the Nazarenes as Paul), broke with his mentor and resigned his earned seat in the Sanhedrin. Those ruptures caused great pain and consternation, for they threatened the stability of Israel's leadership during troubled times.)

Prior to his aligning himself with the condemned sect, Nicodemus (of memory) was known as a man of particularly shrewd business dealings. Not content to live only as heir of his father's prosperous trade route, he revealed unique gifts in increasing his own treasury for many years. But now, at his death, the exact status of Nicodemus' (of memory) remaining wealth is uncertain.

When speaking of the passing of Nicodemus (of memory),

former colleague Ephraim ben Zadok said, "Yes, I felt a great sense of personal loss at the rupture of the Sanhedrin by his choice to join with the followers of the heretic prophet and foment messianism. His resignation was appropriate, but painful. Even though his choices have made him one of those who now threaten the very existence of Israel, I personally was grieved at the news of his sudden death. He was a man of incomparable ability in finance and diplomacy. His keen mind was exceedingly shrewd, but generous. Israel lost a great talent, and now his sect has lost a great pillar."

The son of Jehuda's generosity has been legendary throughout Judea. Recently the focus of his gifts has been upon those who call themselves the "followers of the Way." The sect seems to have no firm structure, but many have said that Nicodemus' wealth has supported many widows. His generosity has also assisted those who lost their livelihood because they chose to follow a crucified leader.

Two days ago Yochanin of Capernaum commented vehemently in the Sanhedrin on Nicodemus' death. "I speak today of the apparent groundswell of misapplied loyalty over old friendships with a former member of this body, Nicodemus (may his name be stricken from memory). I have no patience with the emotions that seem to grant some acceptance of and support to this outlawed group. The sympathies expressed by some of this body may yet tear the very fabric of Israel.

"Our very traditions are under siege. First we were caught between the threat of Babylon and Egypt. Then we found aggression on either side from the Syrians and the Egyptians. Later Parthia and Rome squeezed us. Now we have Rome all around us and this growing decay from within. That man chose to join those who corrupt Israel. The price of our chosenness has always put us between two paws, and the death of one such as Nicodemus (may his name be stricken from memory) represents to me no loss in Israel. May all our enemies be as that man!"

It appears that much, if not all, of the wealth of the house of Jehuda has vanished because of Nicodemus' generous support of the heretic sect that he embraced so fully. One of the leading Nazarene followers, a Simon ben Micah (now imprisoned in the lower-level cells of the home of the high priest), is said to have stated, "I do believe that Nicodemus may have died completely without resources. But in spite of his poverty and great age, he seemed to find joy in his faith and died, I am sure, a uniquely fulfilled man."

The former leader is mourned by two daughters and unnumbered people of Jerusalem who received benefit of his generosity. Only the years will tell if Nicodemus (of memory) will be forgotten because of his choices of allegiance.